A DEADLY MEETING

"What do you want?" Chiun asked.

"Your destruction," said the nurse.

"Why?" said Chiun.

"Because while you live you are a danger to me."

"We can share the earth."

"I am not here to share the earth. I am here to survive," said the nurse. "You two represent a force that has been continuing for centuries and centuries. And you are the one force I must destroy."

But Chiun and Remo had other plans . . .

Destroyer Series:

#1 CREATED, THE DESTROYER
#2 DEATH CHECK
#3 CHINESE PUZZLE
#4 MAFIA FIX
#5 DR. QUAKE
#6 DEATH THERAPY
#7 UNION BUST
#8 SUMMIT CHASE
#9 MURDER'S SHIELD
#10 TERROR SQUAD
#11 KILL OR CURE
#12 SLAVE SAFARI
#13 ACID ROCK
#14 JUDGMENT DAY
#15 MURDER WARD
#16 OIL SLICK
#17 LAST WAR DANCE
#18 FUNNY MONEY
#19 HOLY TERROR
#20 ASSASSINS PLAY-OFF
#21 DEADLY SEEDS
#22 BRAIN DRAIN

The Destroyer

BRAIN DRAIN #22

by Richard Sapir & Warren Murphy

PINNACLE BOOKS • NEW YORK CITY

This is a work of fiction. All the characters and events portrayed in this book are fictional, and any resemblance to real people or incidents is purely coincidental.

THE DESTROYER: BRAIN DRAIN

Copyright © 1976 by Richard Sapir and Warren Murphy

All rights reserved, including the right to reproduce this book or portions thereof in any form.

An original Pinnacle Books edition, published for the first time anywhere.

ISBN: 0-523-00805-8

First printing, January 1976

Cover illustration by Hector Garrido

Printed in the United States of America

PINNACLE BOOKS, INC.
275 Madison Avenue
New York, N.Y. 10016

For Roxy

who knows that easy means strong—and
most of all for the awesome, magnificence of
the glorious house of Sinanju which sometimes recognizes the Post Office Box 1149,
Pittsfield, Mass., 01201 (twentieth century
only).

BRAIN DRAIN

1

Just outside the door, a rookie patrolman let go of his coffee and cigarette breakfast, all over his blue uniform, then retched up solids from the day before. He could not enter the basement room in Greenwich Village. A New York City detective sergeant helped him back up the iron steps to street level.

Inside the room, a city coroner slipped on the blood and half-flipped onto his back. Getting up, he skidded in the oozing red that had washed over what might once have been a robin's-egg-blue rug. The back of his checkered coat was soaked dark where he had landed. His knees, where he had leaned, were red pads. His hands were red, and he couldn't use his notebooks. The room smelled like the inside of a cow's belly. Excrement and intestines.

Manhattan's chief of homicide detectives, Jake

Waldman, saw the young patrolman outside, dry-heaving over a fire hydrant, with one of his detectives holding him steady.

"Too much for the kid?" asked Inspector Waldman.

"Too much for anyone," said the detective.

"A stiff's a stiff. Only the living hurt you," said Inspector Waldman to the rookie, who nodded respectfully between heaves. The detective nodded, too.

He had once seen Waldman talking away in a room with a month-old stiff that would have made a rhinoceros gag, the cigar bouncing around his lips, while other men left because they had to get a breath of breatheable air or go insane. Waldman had a stomach of boilerplate iron. He would eat pastrami sandwiches, dripping with delicatessen cole slaw, in the city morgue and wonder why other people thought this peculiar.

When Willie "Grapes" Riggi got it with two Bren guns all over his face at Gigliotti's Clam House on Mulberry Street, a coroner found a trace of potato salad and mustard in what was left of the eye socket and commented that Waldman must have seen the body already. He had.

"Tomato juice and pickles, kid. It'll fix you right up," said Inspector Waldman, his thick square face nodding with fatherly concern, his cigar bobbing up and down for emphasis.

At this, the rookie cop flailed wildly in another dry heave.

"What'd I say?" asked Waldman. People were always reacting strangely.

He was glad the press wasn't here yet. Television

had its own crazy rules. He had been a detective when TV news was first coming in, and one day he'd seen a departmental directive ordering that "such detectives and other police personnel shall not, *repeat* NOT, consume candy bars or any other sweets, nourishments, condiments, or beverages at homicide scenes, since television reportage of the above-said masticatory acts tends to promote an image of departmental insensitivity toward the deceased."

"What's that supposed to mean?" young Waldman had asked a full detective sergeant. He knew that good police writing could be measured by how many times a person had to use a dictionary to decipher it. It would be years before he could write like that, let alone speak to reporters like that.

"It means, Waldy, that you shouldn't have eaten that potato knish over that mutilated nun's body in front of the television cameras yesterday."

Waldman had shrugged. He never had understood Catholicism too well. Now, years later, watching the rookie struggle for air over the hydrant, he was glad the television cameras hadn't arrived yet. He had just bought a fresh, salted pretzel and he didn't want it to get cold in his pocket.

Waldman saw the coroner stumble up the steps leading from the basement, his hands and knees bloodied, his eyes wide in shock.

"Hey, get a doctor," yelled Waldman to the detective helping the rookie.

"Doctors have been here and left," the detective yelled back. "They're all dead inside."

"We've got a hurt man here. The coroner," said Waldman.

3

"It's not my blood," said the coroner.

"Oh," said Waldman. He saw a press car weave behind the police barricade down the street and quickly finished his pretzel, stuffing the last chunk into an already-full mouth. He just wouldn't talk for a minute, that was all.

Going down the iron steps, he saw the coroner had left bloody footprints. The little cement well before the door smelled of fresh urine, despite the cold March rain of the day before. The small drain in the center of the well was clogged with the soot that collected in all open water in the city. The coroner had left bloody prints on the door. What was the matter with these people? This was a murder scene and you weren't supposed to go touching things. Everyone was acting like rookies. Waldman poked the green, paint-chipped wooden door open, using the rubber end of a pencil. A large grain of salt from the pretzel caught in a lower right tooth. It hurt. It would disappear when he could get his mouth empty enough to suck it out.

The door creaked open and Waldman stepped gingerly inside, looking to avoid the blood pools and chewing rapidly. There were no dry islands. The floor rippled with human blood, a small wall-to-wall lake, slippery red. A white 150-watt bulb suspended from the ceiling was reflected in the red slick. To his right, a head looked dumbly up at him from a couch pillow, its right ear just a dark hole near a bloody temple. A pile of bloody pants seemed entangled under a small wrought-iron table at the far end of the room. Waldman looked closer. There was no body attached to them. Closer. It was three legs. Differ-

4

ent shoes. Three different shoes. At least three deaths.

The room smelled of released body smells, with an overtone of sticky-sweet hashish. But it was not the smell that did it.

Waldman stopped chewing and spat the pretzel out of his mouth.

"Oh," he said. "Oh. Wow. *Oh*."

He had seen the walls. Cement block covered with random psychedelic posters. A kid's pad, or an artist's. But no pad in Greenwich Village ever had walls like this, walls that dripped small lines of blood. Walls with holes that human arms stuck out from, right near the ceiling. It looked as if the walls had arms. A pinky was contracted on an arm that had only ceiling molding for an armpit.

Death was death, and raw death was raw death, but this stepped beyond. Not in his years of picking floaters out of the East River or even bodies from garbage dumps where rats gnawed their way inside to feast had he seen something like this. Death was death. But *this*? And above the doorway in the plaster ceiling, were embedded the blood-drained trunks of four bodies. Three male. One female.

The room darkened, and Waldman felt himself becoming light, but he kept his balance and made his way out the door again, where he breathed deep the blessed stench of natural city air. Years of training and using his common sense took over. He got the police photographers in and out quickly, warning them beforehand that they had a horror ahead of them and that they should do their job as quickly, and especially as mechanically, as they could.

5

The photographs would place the parts of bodies where they had been in the room. He personally tagged limb and head and random organs on a large chart of the room. He placed a limp eyeball in a clear plyofilm bag and labeled it. He got two detectives to question people in the building, another to track down the landlord. He had interns from nearby St. Vincent's Hospital help detectives to unwedge the remnants of people from the walls and ceiling.

The butchered pieces were brought to the morgue. It was when they tried to reassemble the bodies for identification, which he knew by sight would be impossible—only fingerprints and dental work could identify these leavings—that he discovered the other beyond-reason element in a slaughter he had already stamped in his mind as beyond reason. The chief coroner was the first to point it out.

"Your people forgot to pick up something."

"What?"

"Look at the skulls."

The brains had been scraped out. "It was such a mess in there," said Waldman.

"Yeah. But where are the brains?"

"They must be here," said Waldman.

"Your people get everything?" asked the coroner.

"Yeah. We're even cleaning up now."

"Well, the brains are missing."

"They've got to be here somewhere. What about those bags full of gook?" asked Waldman.

"The gook, as you call it, includes everything but the brains."

"Then that organ of the deceased bodies was

6

transported from the premises of the homicide by the perpetrator," said Waldman.

"That's right, Inspector," said the coroner. "Somebody took the brains."

At the press conference Inspector Waldman had to tell a *Daily News* reporter three times that the organs of the deceased that were missing were not the organs that the reporter thought they were. "Brains, if you really want to know," said Waldman.

"Shit," said the *Daily News* reporter. "There goes a great story. Not that this isn't good. But it could have been great."

Waldman went home to his Brooklyn apartment without having dinner. Thinking about the homicide, he had trouble sleeping. He had thought he had seen it all, but this was beyond ... beyond ... beyond what? Not reason really. Reason had patterns. Someone, obviously with power tools, had taken apart human beings. That was a pattern. And the removal of the brains, no matter how disgusting, was a pattern. The arms in the walls, but not the legs, were part of the pattern. And so were the trunks of the bodies.

It must have taken a good two hours to whack out the crevices in the ceiling and the walls and to insert the bodies properly. But where were the tools? And if it did take two hours or even an hour, why was there only one set of bloody footprints when he had entered. The rookie cop had taken one look at the doorway and been escorted up by a detective. The first doctors to arrive had just looked inside the room and made a blanket pronouncement of death.

Only the coroner's footprints were on the stairs when Waldman went in. How had the killer or killers left without leaving bloody footprints?

"Hey, Jake, come to bed," said Waldman's wife.

Waldman looked at his watch. It was 2:30 A.M.

"At this hour, Ethel?"

"I mean to sleep," said his wife. "I can't sleep without you near me."

So Inspector Jake Waldman slid under the quilt with his wife, felt her snuggle to him, and stared at the ceiling.

Assuming the homicides were rational, because of the pattern, what was the reason for the pattern? Arms in walls and bodies in ceilings. Brains removed.

"Hey, Jake," said Mrs. Waldman.

"What?"

"If you're not going to sleep, get out of bed."

"Make up your mind," said Waldman.

"Go to sleep," said Ethel.

"I am. I'm thinking."

"Stop thinking and go to sleep."

"How do you stop thinking?"

"You drop dead already."

Jake Waldman sucked the last small fragment of salt from his right lower molar.

In the morning, Ethel Waldman noticed that her husband didn't touch the bagels, only picked at the lox with onions and eggs, and hardly bothered to sip his cup of tea.

"There's something wrong with the food already?" she asked.

"No. I'm thinking."

8

"Still thinking? You were thinking last night. How long are you thinking?"

"I'm thinking."

"You don't like my eggs."

"No. I like your eggs."

"You like my eggs so much you're letting them turn to stone."

"It's not your eggs. I'm thinking."

"There's another woman," said Ethel Waldman.

"Woman, *shwoman*, what other woman?" asked Waldman.

"I knew it. There's someone else," said Ethel Waldman. "Someone who doesn't ruin her nails cooking for you or get wrinkles worrying about how to make you happy. Some little street chippie with cheap perfume and a young set of boobs who doesn't care beans about you like I care. I know."

"What are you talking about?"

"I hope you and that cheap tart you're running around with are very happy. Get out of here. Get out of here."

"C'mon, Ethel, I got problems."

"Get out of here, animal. Go to your whore. Go to your whore."

"I've got work. I'll see you tonight, Ethel."

"Get out. Out, animal."

And in the hallway of the fifth floor of their apartment building, Jake Waldman heard his wife yell out to the world:

"Lock up your daughters, everyone. The whoremaster's on the loose."

At the division headquarters, there was a phone call waiting for Inspector Waldman. It was Ethel. She would do anything to patch up their marriage.

9

They should try again. Like adults. She would forget the incident with the actress.

"What actress? What incident?"

"Jake. If we're trying again, let's at least be honest."

"All right, all right," said Waldman, who had been through this before.

"Was she a famous actress?"

"Ethel!"

And that held the family problems for the day. The mayor's office wanted a special report and the commissioner's office wanted a special report and some agency in Washington wanted some kind of report for a special study and a psychologist from Wayne State University wanted to talk to Waldman, so Inspector Waldman hauled the lowest grade detective he saw first and gave him an assignment.

"Keep those dingbats off my back," he said.

The police photographers had come up with something interesting. Perhaps Waldman had missed it during the rush to finish up the on-the-scene work. But could he make out a certain poster on the wall through the lines of blood? Right under that arm there?

"*Hmmmm*," said Waldman.

"What do you think?" asked the photographer.

"I think I'm going back to that basement. Thank you."

"Crazy, huh?" said the photographer.

"No. Reasonable," said Waldman.

There were knots of people around the basement apartment, both attracted but kept at a distance by the police barricades. The rookie had apparently recovered well because he looked professional and bored standing in front of the iron steps leading to the basement.

"I told you it was nothing, kid," commented Waldman going down the steps.

"Yeah, nothing," said the rookie cockily.

"You'll be picking up eyeballs in plyofilm bags in no time and thinking nothing of it, kid," said Waldman, noticing the rookie double over and run toward the curb. Funny kid.

The basement room now smelled like a sharp commercial disinfectant. The rug was gone and the floor was scrubbed, but much of the brown stain could not be scrubbed away. It had soaked into the wooden floor. That was strange. Basement apartments usually had cement floors. Waldman hadn't noticed the construction before because of the blood. Funny how much new blood was like oil, a slippery coating when first spilled.

Waldman took the photograph out of the manila envelope, tearing off the little silver snap that went through the hole in the flap. The disinfectant rose beyond smell. It was a taste now. Like swallowing a mothball.

The glossy photograph reflected the harsh light from the bulb overhead. The room felt surprisingly cool, even for a basement. He looked at the photograph, then looked at the wall. The wall posters had been scraped during the cleaning process and now were only barely discernible strips.

But he had the photograph. And between the photograph and the small strips left on the wall, he saw it. On the wall there had been a surrealistic poster of a room. And from the walls of that room hung

11

arms. And in the ceilings were trunks of bodies. And looking at the photograph of what the poster had been and at the remnants of the poster now, Inspector Waldman saw that the room had been made into a replica of this mad poster. Almost exactly in proportion to the picture. It was an imitation of the picture. He stepped back on the creaking floor. An exact, proportional, almost slavish imitation. He felt something about this, and his instinct told him it was important. What was it?

Waldman looked down at the photograph again. Sure. That was it. There was no deviation from the poster at all. The room had reproduced the horror of the poster exactly, almost as if the killer had been programmed to do it, almost as if he had no feelings of his own. It was as if a mindless ape had imitated art and created nothing but death.

Of course, none of this could go in a report. He'd be laughed out of the department. But he wondered what sort of killers could remain calm enough to exactly copy a poster during the hysteria of mass murder. Probably a devil cult of some sort. In that case, there would be more of these, and the perpetrators were doomed. Almost anyone had a fair chance of getting away with something once. Sometimes twice. But something like this they would have to do again, and when they got to the third time, or maybe even the second, some circumstance, some accident of performance, some loose word somewhere, some left wallet, some random thing, like even a door locking behind them or being seen in the act, would get them. Time, not brilliance, was the law's edge.

Waldman stepped back. One of the boards on the

floor was loose. The place shouldn't have had a wooden floor anyhow. He stamped down hard on one end of the board. The other rose, like a brown-stained square tongue. He leaned down and ripped it up. It covered small plastic bags with oblong brown wads slightly smaller than Hershey bars. So that was the reason for the flooring. Waldman smelled the contents of a bag. Hashish. He kicked off the board next to the first. More bags. The basement was a stash. In rough estimates, he saw about thirty-five hundred dollars worth already. He kicked over another board. Where he had expected to find bags, Waldman saw an oblong tape deck, with a small dim yellow light in the control panel. The spool spun around and around, whipping a liver-colored end of tape against the gray plastic edge of a panel. He stared at it going around, the tape softly whipping the panel edge. He saw a black cord lead through a drilled hole in the wooden floor support. The machine was on record.

He pressed stop, rethreaded the spool and put the machine on rewind. The tape spun back rapidly. The machine had belonged to the dealer. Many pushers had them. A tape could help give them protection. It could raise a little blackmail money. It had many uses.

Before the tape rewound completely, he pressed stop again. Then play.

"Hello, hello, hello. I'm so glad you're all here." The voice was silky high, like a drag queen's. "I suppose you're all wondering, wondering, wondering what lovelies I have for you."

"Money, man." This voice was heavier and deeper. "Bread, baby. The mean green."

13

"Of course, lovelies. I wouldn't deprive you of sustenance."

"For a dealer, that's the level truth. Totally level." A girl's voice.

"Hush, hush, lovelies. I'm an artist. I just do other things to live. Besides, the walls have ears."

"You probably put 'em there, mother."

"Hush, hush. No negativities in front of my guest."

"He the one that want something?"

"Yes, he does. His name is Mr. Regal. And he has given me money for you all. Much money. Lovely money."

"And we ain't gonna see but a spit of it."

"There's plenty for you. He wants you to do something in front of him. No, Marla, don't take off your clothes. That's not what he wants. Mr. Regal wants you, as artists, to share your creativity with him."

"What's he doin' with the pipe?"

"I told him that hash helps creativity."

"That dude be goin' through a full ounce. He gotta be blind now."

And then the voice. That chilling flat monotone. Waldman felt a cramp in his legs from kneeling down near the tape. Where had he heard a voice like that before?

"I am not intoxicated, if that is what you suspect. Rather, I have full control of my senses and reflexes. Perhaps this inhibits my creativity. That is why I smoke more than the normal amount, or what you would consider normal, man."

"You jive funny, turkey."

"That is a derogatory term, and I have found that

14

for one to tolerate such language often leads to further abuses of one's territorial integrity. Therefore, desist, nigger."

"Now, now, now, lovelies. Let us make pretty. Each of you will show your art to Mr. Regal. Let him see what you do when you are creative."

The tape sounded blank except for shuffling feet. Waldman heard indistinguishable low mumblings. Someone asked for "the red," which Waldman assumed was paint. At one point, someone sang an off-key tune about oppression and how freedom was just another form of deprivation and that the singer needed copulation badly with whomever she was singing to, but she didn't want her head messed with. "Just My Body, Baby" seemed to be the title of the song.

The flat voice again. "Now I noted that the painter seemed highly calm when working, and the singer seemed aroused. Is there an explanation for this, faggot?"

"I hate that word, but everything is so lovely I'll ignore it. Yes, there is a reason. All creativity comes from the heart. While the face and sounds may be different, the heart, the lovely heart, is the center of the creative process, Mr. Regal."

"Incorrect." That flat far-away voice again. "The brain sends all creative signals. The body itself— liver, kidney, intestines or heart—plays no part in the creative process. Do not lie to me, queer."

"Hmmmm. Well, I see you're into an insulting bag. Heart is only a phrase. Hardly do we mean a body organ. Heart is that essence of creativity. Physically, of course, it comes from the brain."

"Which part of the brain?"

15

"I don't know."

"Continue."

Waldman heard a heavy banging of feet and assumed it was a dance. Then there was a chopping sound.

"Sculpture, lovelies, might be the ultimate art."

"It looks like a male reproductive organ." The flat voice.

"That's a work of art, too. You'd know, if you ever tasted it." Giggle. The fag.

There were a few mumbled requests to pass a pipe, probably filled with hashish.

"Well, there you have it." The fag.

"Have what?" The flat voice.

"Creativity. A song. A dance. A painting. A piece of sculpture. Perhaps you would like to try, Mr. Regal? What would you like to do? You must remember of course that to be creative you must do something different. Difference is the essence of creativity. Come on now, Mr. Regal. Do something different."

"Other than sculpture and dancing and painting and singing?"

"Oh yes, that would be lovely." The fag.

"I don't know what to do." The flat voice.

"Well, let me give you a hint. Often the beginning of creativity is copying what's already been done, but in a different way. You build creativity by copying in a different medium. For instance, you change a painting into a sculpture. Or vice versa. Look around. Find something and then change it into a different medium."

And suddenly there were screams and awful tearing sounds, cracking bones and joints that came

16

apart like thick, soft balloons stretched too far. And the wild desperate screams of the singer.

"No, no, no, no. *No!*" It was a wail, it was a chant, it was a prayer. And it wasn't answered. *Snap! Pop!* And there were no more screams. Waldman heard the heavy crunch of plaster, and it hit the ground with a splash. Probably in a pool of blood. Plaster, then splash.

"Lovely." The flat voice. This time it echoed through the room. Then the door closed on the tape.

Inspector Waldman rewound the tape to where the screaming had begun. He played it forward, watching the second hand of his watch. A minute and a half. All that done by one man. In eighty-five seconds.

Waldman rewound the tape and played it back. It had to be one man. There were the voices of the four victims and their references to their guest, their one guest. He listened carefully. It sounded like power tools at work but he did not hear any motors. Eighty-five seconds.

Waldman stumbled trying to straighten up. He had been kneeling too long for his fifty-year-old frame. You knew you were getting old when you couldn't do that anymore. A young patrolman with a happy, glad-to-meet-you smile entered the basement room.

"Yeah?" said Waldman. The patrolman's face was familiar. Then he saw the badge. Of course. It must have been the model for the recruiting poster. Looked just like him, right down to that artificial friendly grin. But that couldn't be a real badge. The commercial artist hired by the police department, some radical freak, had done his defiance bit by giving the poster model a badge number no one had ... "6969" which meant an obscenity.

And this patrolman, now smiling at Waldman, had that number.

"Who are you?"

"Patrolman Gilbys, sir." That flat voice. It was the voice on the tape.

"Oh, good," said Waldman pleasantly. "Good."

"I heard you were on the case."

"Oh, yeah," said Waldman. He would put the suspect at ease, then casually get him to the station house, and stick a revolver in his face. Waldman tried to remember when he had last cleaned his pistol. A year and a half ago. No matter. A police special could take all sorts of abuse.

"I was wondering what you meant by a horror scene? You were quoted as such in the newspapers. You didn't mention creativity. Did you think it was creative?"

"Sure, sure. Most creative thing I've ever seen. All the guys down at the station house thought it was a work of art. You know, we ought to go down and talk to them about it."

"I do not know if you are aware of it, but your voice is modulating unevenly. This is a sure indication of lying. Why do you lie to me, kike? I assume it is kike, unless, of course, it is kraut."

"Lie? Who's lying? It *was* creative."

"You will tell me the truth, of course. People talk through pain," said the phony patrolman with the glad-to-meet-you smile and the obscene badge from the recruiting poster.

Waldman stepped back, reaching for his gun, but the patrolman's hand was squeezing his eyeballs.

His hands couldn't move and in the red, blinding pain, Waldman told the patrolman the truth. It was the most uncreative horror Waldman had ever seen.

"Thank you," said the phony patrolman. "I took it right from the poster, but I did not think copying someone else's work was creative. Thank you." Then, like a drill press, he pushed his right hand through Waldman's heart until it met his left hand.

"So much for constructive criticism," the flat voice said.

2

His name was Remo and they wanted him to show his press pass. They wanted him to do this so much that Brother George stuck the barrel of a Kalishnikov automatic rifle under his right eye and Sister Alexa put a .45 caliber automatic in the small of his back, while Brother Ché stood across the room aiming a Smith and Wesson revolver at his skull.

"If he steps funny, we'll blow him to hamburger," Sister Alexa had said.

No one wondered why this man who said he was a reporter failed to be surprised when the hotel room door opened. No one suspected that just not talking while waiting for him was not enough silence, that tense breathing could be heard even through a door as thick as that one in the Bay State Motor Inn, West Springfield, Mass. He seemed like such an ordinary man. Thin, just under six feet tall, with high cheekbones. Only his thick wrists might have told them something. He seemed so casual in his gray slacks and black turtleneck sweater and soft, glove-leather loafers.

"Let's see it," said Brother Ché as Brother George closed the door behind him.

"I have it somewhere," said Remo reaching into his right pocket. He saw Brother George's right index finger squeeze very close on the trigger, perhaps closer to firing than Brother George knew. Sweat beaded on Brother George's forehead. His lips were chapped and dry. He drew air into his lungs with short choppy breaths that seemed to just replenish the tip of his supply of oxygen, as though he dared not risk a complete exhale.

Remo produced a plastic-covered police shield issued by the New York City Police Department.

"Where's the card from the *Times*? This is a police card," said Brother George.

"If he showed you a special card from the *Times*, you should start wondering," said Brother Ché. "All New York papers use cards issued by the police."

"They're a tool of the pig police," said Brother George.

"The cards come from the police so the reporters can get past police lines at fires and things," said Brother Ché. He was a scrawny man, with a bearded face that looked as though it had once been bathed in crankcase oil and would never be fully clean again.

"I don't trust no pig," said Brother George.

"Let's off him," said Sister Alexa. Remo could see her nipples harden under her light white peasant blouse. She was getting her sexual jollies from this.

He smiled at her, and her eyes lowered to her gun. Her pale, pottery-white skin flushed red in the cheeks. Her knuckles were white around the gun, as if she were afraid it would do its own bidding if not held tightly.

Brother Ché got the card from Brother George.

"All right," said Brother Ché. "Do you have the money?"

"I have the money if you have the goods," said Remo.

"How do we know we'll get the money if we show you what we've got?"

"You have me. You have the guns."

"I don't trust him," said Brother George.

"He's all right," said Brother Ché.

"Let's off him now. Now," said Sister Alexa.

"No, no," said Brother Ché, stuffing the Smith and Wesson into his beltless gray pants.

"We can get it all printed ourselves. Every bit of it the way we want," said Sister Alexa. "Let's stick it to him."

"And two hundred people who already think like us will read it," said Brother Ché. "No. The *Times* will make it international knowledge."

"Who cares what someone in Mexico City thinks?" said Sister Alexa.

"I don't trust him," said Brother George.

"A little revolutionary discipline, please," said Brother Ché. He nodded for George to stand by the door and for Alexa to go to the closed bathroom door. The curtains were drawn over the window. It was twelve stories down from the window, Remo knew. Brother Ché nodded for Remo to sit at a small glass-and-chrome coffee table.

Sister Alexa brought a pale, bespectacled man out of the bathroom. She helped him lug a large black cardboard suitcase with new leather straps to the coffee table. He had the wasted look of a man whose only sunshine had come from overhead fluorescent lights.

"Have we gotten the money?" he asked, looking at Brother Ché.

"We will," said Brother Ché.

The pale man opened the case and clumsily put it on the floor.

"I'll explain everything," he said, taking a stack of computer printouts from the suitcase, laying out a manila envelope which proved to have news clippings, and finally a white pad with nothing on it. He clicked a green ballpoint pen into readiness.

"This is the biggest story you're ever going to get," he told Remo. "Bigger than Watergate. Bigger than any assassination. Much bigger than any CIA activity in Chile or the FBI's wiretaps. This is the biggest story happening in America today. And it's a scoop."

"He's already here to buy," said Brother Ché. "Don't waste time."

"I'm a computer operator at a sanitarium on Long Island Sound in Rye, New York. It's called Folcroft. I don't know if you've ever heard of it."

Remo shrugged. The shrug was a lie.

"Do you have pictures of it?" asked Remo.

"Anyone can just walk up and take pictures. You can get pictures," said the man.

"The place is not the point," said Brother Ché.

"Right, I would guess," said the man. "I don't know if you're familiar with computers or not, but you don't need all that much information to program them. Just what's necessary to the core. However, four years ago, I began to do some figuring, right?"

"I guess," said Remo. He had been told it was three years ago that Arnold Quilt, thirty-five, of 1297 Ruvolt Street, Mamaroneck, three children, M.S. 1961 MIT, had started his "peculiar research" and was being watched. The day before, Remo had gotten Arnold Quilt's picture. It did not capture the utter lack of natural light on his face.

"Basically, and I'd guess you want to simplify it this way, I suspected I was being given a minimum of information for my job. Almost a calculated formula to deprive me of any real reference point outside the narrow confines of my job. I later calculated that there were thousands like me and that any function that might lead a person to a fuller understanding of his job was separated in such a way that all cognitive reference was negated."

"In other words, they'd have three people doing what one could do," said Brother Ché, seeing the man called Remo idly glance toward the shaded window. "One person might get to understand a job fully, but if you have three doing it, none of them ever finds out exactly where he fits in."

"Right," said Remo. He saw the tension go out of Sister Alexa's breasts.

"Well, we are separated in a half-dozen lunchrooms, so that people working on the same program do not associate with each other. I ate with a guy who did nothing but calculate grain prices."

"Get to the point," said Brother Ché impatiently.

"The point is the purpose of this Folcroft. And I ·

24

started calculating and looking. I would move to different lunchrooms. I became as friendly with Dr. Smith's secretary—Dr. Smith, he's the director—I became as friendly with her as I could, but she was a stone wall."

He should get to know Smitty, thought Remo, if he really wants to know a stone wall.

"I'm sure the reporter would be more interested in what you found than in how you found it. You can lay that out later. Tell him what you found," said Brother Ché.

"Talk of illegal undercover. There is an organization operating in America today that is like another government. It watches not only crime figures but law-enforcement agencies. Do you wonder where all the leaks are coming from? Why one prosecutor will suddenly turn on his whole political party and start indicting bigwigs and things? Well, look no further. It's this organization. A lot of what this group does is blamed on the CIA and FBI. It is so secret I doubt if more than two or three people know about it. It exposes terrorist rings, it makes sure the police get tougher inside the law. It's like a secret government set up to make the constitution work. A whole government."

"Tell him about the killers. That's news."

"Their killer arm. You would think they would be most vulnerable there, because you'd have ten, twenty, thirty killers roaming around who know what they're doing, right?" said the pallid man.

"Hopefully," said Remo.

"Well, they don't have a whole pack of killers. I can prove it right here," he said, touching a green-striped computer sheet. "There's one killer, and he's connected to more than fifty deaths that I could find. It's incredible the things he can do. Swift in, out, no trace of him. Fingerprints showing up that in no way check out anywhere else. This person is so sure and so quick and so final and so neat that there is nothing like him known in the Western world. He gets into places that are incredible. If I didn't know better, I would swear that this force, which we have listed as R9-1 DES can go up and down building walls." Remo noticed that the man's eyes were lit with that special office-work sort of joy that comes when someone discovers the muffler file is in the Chevrolet folder.

"Anything about his personality?" asked Remo. "Loyal, courageous, competent, leader of men?"

"There was an entry, but I'm not sure it refers to him."

"What was it?" asked Remo.

"Recalcitrant, unstable, and idealistically confused."

"Who fed that into the computer?"

"I'm not sure. I could do further checking, although I haven't been at Folcroft for a week. You see, I'm supposed to be on vacation."

"That's all right," mumbled Remo. "What's your solid proof of this thing?"

"Ah, glad you asked," said the man. "In Tucson, there is a real estate office. At least everyone there thinks they work for a real estate office. They don't know the information they file is beyond the usual. Well, in this Manila envelope is the payroll which corresponds exactly to the Tucson payroll of this organization. Let me show you." And he took a small computer sheet, perhaps three folds, out of the envelope, along with a canceled check stub and placed them on the white paper and drew lines between corresponding figures.

"Now this," said the man, pointing to the Tucson code number, "uncovers this." He pointed to a name. "Which relates to this." He pointed to B277-L(8)-V. "Which assigns this to another program." He pointed to the name uncovered by the Tucson bureau. The name was Walsh.

"So?" said Remo.

The man grinned a fudge sundae sort of smile and produced a newspaper clipping about a Judge Walsh falling or jumping to his death in Los Angeles. Judge Walsh, the clipping pointed out, had given fewer and lighter sentences to suspected drug pushers than any other district court judge.

"How do I know you haven't made a photocopy of the printout?" asked Remo looking closely at the edges of the green-striped computer paper. "I mean you could give a photocopy to the *Washington Post* or the *Kearny Observer* or *Seneca Falls Pennysaver* or something, and there goes our exclusive. And your money."

"Ah, glad you asked. You see this paper? You see the edges? Well, when any photocopy is made of this paper, it turns red at the edges."

"How do I know you didn't use a camera instead of some machine? A camera wouldn't show."

"Look. Do you want it or don't you?" said Brother Ché.

"I suppose that's it," said Remo to Brother Ché, turning with a relaxed smile. "And you, Arnold," he said to the pallid man who had never mentioned his name, "will tell me the truth shortly."

27

Brother George brought up his Kalishnikov, the trigger finger already squeezing. But Remo spun from his chair in a motion so smooth that for the fraction of life the others had left, they would have sworn it was slow. But if it were slow, how did he get behind Brother George and so easily swing the Kalishnikov toward Brother Ché? The burst of fire mottled Brother Ché's gray face with red splotches the size of broken grapes. Sister Alexa tried to get a shot at the man, but all she saw was Brother George protesting his love for her. He was her man.

"I love you," screamed George. "I don't want to kill you," But his finger moved without his control, a hand so placed on his wrist that the hand, not his mind, had control of his fingers. Brother George's first shot clipped off her shoulder because George managed to jerk. It threw her back and, terrified, she unloaded her .45 at her lover. Remo got the arm just right on Brother George and this time he put her away with a burst through the chest. George's stomach was an oozing red cavity where soft .45 slugs cut a churning crazy path.

Arnold Quilt backed into the corner, shaking, not because he had been hit but because he feared he would be. He covered his groin with his hands for protection.

"Arnold," said Remo, holding up Brother George's body with a grip just above the left ribcage and controlling the Kalishnikov with his right hand, "give me any photographs of the Tucson program."

"There are none."

"Then you'll die."

"I swear there are none. None."

"All right," said Remo and since Brother George's right hand no longer responded to the nerves, Remo dropped him, catching the rifle himself. He put Arnold Quilt away with one dull shot. And dropped the gun.

He hated guns. They were so, so ... he had no word for it in English. But in Korean it would be "out of natural control and an intrusion upon grace."

However work was work, and upstairs wanted it to look like a relatively simply homicide. Brother George had gone berserk and killed Arnold Quilt, Brother Ché, and Sister Alexa, who, dying, managed to get her slayer. Remo had not been informed that Brother George and Sister Alexa were lovers, which annoyed him. Upstairs was slipping.

Remo put the gun back in George's still hand and took the tipped section of the Tucson program. He felt sorry for Quilt. Working for Smitty at Folcroft could lead a man to do anything. Then again, he should have gotten along with Smith fine. Computers and Dr. Harold Smith had the same emotional quotient. What did computer expert Arnold Quilt expect from human beings anyway? Humanity?

There would be no trouble with fingerprints. The police might find a strange set on the gun, but no cross reference ever devised could dig up the prints of a man certified dead more than a decade ago, certified by the drunken doctor at the New Jersey State Prison in Trenton, where the man once known as Remo Williams had been electrocuted. After, of course, being neatly framed for a murder he didn't commit. And when Remo Williams came to in a sanitarium, he was offered a new life and he took it.

The name of the sanitarium was Folcroft.

Remo ran out of the hotel room, the computer program safely folded in his pants pockets, screaming: "Murder. Murder. There's been murder. There, down the hall. Murder."

He got into a down elevator with four startled men who were wearing Kiwanis buttons introducing themselves as Ralph, Armand, Phil, and Larry. The buttons said they were glad to meet anyone looking at the buttons.

"What happened?" asked Armand.

"Horrible. Murder. Twelfth floor."

"Any sex in it?" asked Ralph, who was in his late fifties.

"Two of them loved each other."

"I mean, you know, sex," said Ralph.

"You ought to see the bodies," said Remo with a big wink.

When the elevator reached the lobby, Remo left. The four Kiwanians stayed. Ralph pressed twelve.

Remo strolled out into the lobby of soft leather chairs, bathing in the new spring light that beamed through tall street windows. A confused patrolman was talking at the desk to a hysterical clerk.

"Twelfth floor," said Remo. "Four guys saw it all. Big sex scene. They're wearing buttons. They're Ralph, Armand, Phil, and Larry."

"What happened?" asked the patrolman.

"I don't know," said Remo. "Those four guys were just yelling 'murder.'"

An hour and a half away by car was Cape Cod, not yet blossomed into its full tourist season, a town built for summer pleasure and populated during the winter by people who served that pleasure and complained about those who enjoyed it.

Remo saw that the driveway to a small white cottage overlooking the dark foaming Atlantic was empty. He jammed the brakes and let the car skid into the driveway. He did not like using a gun and his body felt and resented it. What police technicians could pick up only with a paraffin test, his body could sense through its nervous system, now so acute that even food seasoned with monosodium glutamate would have the effect of knockout drops. A few years before, when he had still hungered for meat, he had eaten a chain-food special and been hospitalized. The attending physician discovered medically what Remo had known only philosophically: that when something becomes very much different, it becomes something new.

"You don't have a human being's nervous system," the doctor had said.

"Blow it out your stethoscope," Remo had said, but he knew the doctor was right. He had eaten the hamburger not out of the hunger of his body but out of a remembered hunger, and had found what writers always seemed to learn first—you can't go home again.

Remo opened the door to the Cape Cod cottage. The guns still bothered him.

In the center of the living room sat a frail man in lotus position, his golden morning-kimono flowing down around him. Wisps of white hair, like smooth gentle strands of silk, played from his temples and chin. The television set was turned on and Remo sat respectfully waiting for "As the Planet Revolves" to come to a commercial so he could speak his mind to the old man, Chiun.

Fourteen ancient lacquered trunks stood packed against a far wall, seeming almost to wait their own turn to speak.

"Disgusting," said Chiun when a commercial came on. "They have ruined great dramas with violence and sex."

"Little Father," said Remo, "I don't feel very well."

"Did you breathe this morning?"

"I breathed."

"Properly?"

"Of course."

"It is when one says 'of course' to anything that one loses what he takes for granted," said Chiun. "It is not uncommon for one to squander the greatest wealth in the world by not watching it. You alone have been given the teaching of Sinanju and therefore the powers of Sinanju. Do not lose them through improper breathing."

"It was proper. It was proper," said Remo. "I used a gun."

The two long-fingered hands opened in an offering of innocence. "Then what would you want of me?" Chiun asked. "I give you diamonds, and you prefer to play with mud."

"I wanted to share my feelings with you."

"Share your good feelings. Keep the bad for yourself," said Chiun and in Korean he spoke about the inability of even one so great as the Master of Sinanju to transform mud into diamonds or a pale piece of pig's ear into something of worth, and what was even the Master to do when an ingrate came back with handfuls of mud and complained that it did not sparkle like diamonds?

"Shared feelings," mumbled Chiun in English. "Do I share a belly ache? I share wisdom. You share stomach pains."

"You never had a belly ache," said Remo, but he stopped talking as soon as "As the Planet Revolves" resumed. The shows were basically the same as a few years before, but now they had blacks and abortions and people no longer looked longingly at each other; they shared a bed. Yet it was still attenuated gossip, even though its star was none other than Rad Rex, whose autographed picture Chiun carried wherever he went.

Remo saw a country cleanup crew ride past in a pickup truck. A banner announcing a bicentennial art exhibit fluttered from the side panels. Chiun got along with the local people well. Remo felt like an outsider. Chiun had told him that he would always be an outsider until he recognized that his true home was Sinanju, the tiny village in North Korea from which Chiun came, and not America, where Remo was born.

"To understand others you must first realize they are others, and not just you with a different face," Chiun had said. They had been living in the house only a week when Chiun explained the hostility local people always felt toward tourists.

"It is not their wealth they resent or that they come for the most pleasant of seasons. It is that a tourist will always say goodbye and goodbyes are little deaths. So they cannot like anyone too much for they will be hurt. The problem is not that they dislike tourists but that they are afraid to like them, for fear of hurt when parting."

"You don't understand Americans, Little Father."

"What is there to understand? I know they do not appreciate fine assassins, but have amateurs practicing hither and yon, and their great dramas have been ruined by evil men who wish only to sell things to wash garments. There is nothing to understand."

"I have seen Sinanju now, Little Father, remember. So don't go talking about the wonders of North Korea and your own little bit of heaven by the bay. I've seen it. It smells like a sewer."

Chiun had looked surprised.

"Now you tell me that you don't like it. You loved it when you were there."

"Loved it? I almost got killed. You almost got killed. I just didn't complain is all."

"For you, that is loving it," Chiun had said, and that had closed the subject.

Now Remo sat back waiting for a commercial. He looked out the window. Down the road came a dark green Chevrolet with New York license plates. The car drove exactly at a thirty-five-mile-per-hour speed that would bore most people into sleeping at the wheel. The speed limit was thirty-five miles per hour. The exact speed of the car, around curves as well as on straightaways, never varying, told Remo who was driving it. He went outside to the driveway shutting the door quietly behind him.

"Hi, Smitty," said Remo to the driver, a lemony-faced man in his fifties, with pursed tight lips and a dehydrated face that had never been moistened by emotion.

34

"Well?" said Dr. Harold W. Smith.

"Well what?" said Remo, stopping him from entering the cottage. Smith could not enter quietly enough not to disturb Chiun while the shows were on, for although he was still athletically trim of body, his mind let his feet clop in the normal Western walk. Chiun had often complained to Remo about these interruptions after Smith had left. He did not need the aggravation of verbal abuse from Chiun today; he felt bad enough about using a gun.

"The job," Smith said. "Did it come off well?"

"No. They got me first."

"I don't need sarcasm, Remo. This one was very important."

"You mean the other jobs were vacations?"

"I mean if you didn't do this one right we will have to close shop, and we're so close to success."

"We're always close to success. We've been close to success for more than ten years now. But it never comes."

"We're in the social tremors preceding improvement. It's to be expected."

"Bullshit," said Remo, who a decade before had come out of a coma in Folcroft and been told of the secret organization named CURE, headed by Dr. Harold W. Smith, designed to make the Constitution work, a quiet little group that would insure the nation's survival against anarchy or a police state. At first Remo had believed. He had become CURE's killer arm, trained by Chiun, the Master of Sinanju, the world's greatest assassin, and he had believed. But he had lost count now of the people he had eliminated who would have made the quiet little group known as CURE into an unquiet big organization.

35

The four in the Bay State Motor Inn were just the latest.

Remo handed Smith the Tucson program.

"Good," said Smith, putting it in his jacket pocket.

"It hasn't been photographed either," said Remo. "You forgot to mention photograph copy."

"Oh, they can't photograph this kind of paper."

"What do you mean by that?"

"Can't be done."

"How do you do that?" asked Remo.

"None of your business."

"Thanks," said Remo.

"It has to do with light waves. Are you happy now?" said Smith. He wore an immaculate gray suit with starched white shirt and that gruesome Dartmouth tie that never seemed to collect a grease spot. Then again, Smith didn't eat grease. He was a turnip and boiled cod kind of person.

"Okay," said Remo. "The commercials are on."

"Can you really hear through walls?"

"None of your business," said Remo.

"How do you do that?"

"You refine quietness. Are you happy now?" said Remo.

Chiun rose to greet Smith, his arms outstretched in salutation.

"Hail, Emperor Smith, whose beneficence and wisdom accommodates the very universe of man. May you live long forever, and may your kingdom be feared throughout the land."

"Thank you," said Smith, looking at the trunks. He had long ago given up trying to tell Chiun that he was not an emperor and not only didn't wish to

36

be feared throughout the land but didn't even want to be known. To this, Chiun had responded that it was an emperor's right to be known or not known as he wished.

"Well, I see you're packed," said Smith. "I wish you and Remo bon voyage, and I will see you again in two months, correct?"

"You will see us with more love for your awesome wisdom, oh, Emperor," said Chiun.

"Where are we going?" said Remo.

"You should know. It's your illness that's sending you there," said Smith.

"Where? What illness?" said Remo.

"You do not remember how badly you felt this morning?" asked Chiun. "You have so quickly forgotten your ill feelings?"

"Oh, that. Well, that was because of the gun thing," said Remo.

"Do not mask pain, lest you deceive your body of proper warnings," Chiun said.

"That was this morning. Those trunks have been packed for a week," Remo said.

"You ought to see Iran if you want to go so badly," Smith said.

"I don't want to go to fucking Iran," Remo said. "It's Chiun who's always talking about Persia."

"You see how his memory is beginning to fail," Chiun said. "He even forgot the other day how he loved Sinanju."

"Hey, wait a minute," Remo said.

"Bon voyage," said Smith. "I see Chiun's show is resuming."

"It is nothing compared to your beauty, Emperor Smith."

37

"Well, thank you," said Smith, succumbing briefly to the flattery that Sinanju assassins had been applying for centuries to many emperors around the globe.

"What's going on here?" Remo asked.

Chiun returned to watching television and Smith left, the Tucson program, the dangerous link to the secrets of CURE, safely in his jacket pocket. Smith drove into the quaint heart of the seashore resort town and stopped by a large aluminum statue that was somehow appealing to him. Everyone else seemed to think it lacked life ... lacked, there was no other phrase for it, a sense of creativity. Smith thought it was just fine. He went closer to look. He saw only the flash of light. He did not see the shards of exploding metal which tore into his insides and made everything very yellow before the world became black.

The explosion was heard in the little white cottage Smith had just left.

The commercials were on again, so Chiun commented: "Is this your Fourth of July? If so, why did I not see many fat women with children?"

"No," said Remo. "How come you didn't complain about Smitty interrupting your show?"

"Complain to an emperor?" said Chiun, shocked. "It was your job to see that he left before my meager pleasures were intruded upon. I was left without your help when I needed it most."

"You didn't miss anything. You could come back to one of those shows five years from now, and you wouldn't miss anything. Rad Rex will still be wearing that silly doctor's smock, still trying to discover a serum that can teach him how to act."

But Chiun was rock silent. The commercials fed into the soap opera and he folded his long fingernails and like a gently settling petal lowered himself to the floor.

The two stars of this soap opera, Val Valerie and Raught Regan were talking in bed. They were not married.

"Disgusting," said Chiun, and he did not talk again until late afternoon when all his shows were over. By then, Remo had heard that a man was seriously injured in town. A little boy on a bicycle shared the gossip.

"Yeah. He was a doctor, too. From New York. The police said he ran a sanitarium there in someplace that's named after bread."

"Whole wheat sanitarium?" Remo said.

The boy shook his head.

"Rye?" said Remo.

"That's right. He ran a sanitarium in Rye."

3

The hospital smelled of ether traces and constant scrubbing. The woman at the information desk said yes, a gentleman had been admitted in serious condition. Yes, the explosion victim. His wife had been notified. The name was Dr. Harold Smith, and no, Remo could not be allowed to see him because he was in the intensive care unit.

Remo smiled boyishly, told the plump middle-aged information woman that she had beautiful eyes, caught her left hand like a fluttering bird and then, as if he were absentminded, moved the pads of his fingertips sensuously along the underside of her wrist. They looked into each other's eyes and discussed the weather and the hospital, and Remo saw a red flush creep up her neck.

In the middle of her halting dissertation on the coming Cape Cod summer, she allowed that while the young man couldn't get permission to enter the intensive care unit, no one ever stopped anyone from entering if he just walked in wearing a white coat. There were white coats in the laundry in the basement and no one ever stopped anyone from taking laundry. Where was the young man going? Would he be back? She was getting off work at eight o'clock. They could meet in a motel. If not a motel, then a car in the parking lot. What about a stairwell? An elevator?

For some reason, the laundry room was locked. Remo pressured the handle straight back, and the door popped open. The pressure looked as though he merely pushed open an unlocked door. He stepped into hospital whites and was out in the hallway looking for ICU. He rode an elevator up with two nurses and an X-ray technician. One of the nurses gave him one of those smiles. Why was it, thought Remo, that now that he had this sort of attraction, he didn't have that strong desire to make any use of it? What he could have done with his Sinanju training when he was eighteen.

Smith was under a tent, tubes going into his nostrils, the left side of his head in gauze and sanitary white tape. He breathed heavily but not without the solid life throb of a body waging a successful struggle for its existence. He would be all right.

"Smitty," said Remo softly. "Smitty."

Smith opened his right eye.

"Hello," he said.

"Hello yourself, dummy. What happened?"

"I don't know," Smith said. "Where are my clothes?"

"You're not going anywhere," Remo said, looking

41

at the tubes running to tanks beside the bed. It was as if Smith himself were a part of this bed unit and to move him would rip him away from his life support system.

"I know that," Smith said. "The Tucson program was in my jacket pocket."

"I'll get it. I'll get it. How did this happen?"

"Well, there was this very tasteful piece of sculpture in the town square. Sort of a bicentennial art celebration, and I went close to examine it. Really very nice, and then it exploded."

"Sounds like some sort of trap. You think there's some connection with the people at Bay State?"

"No, no. They were just another group of disturbeds, who got together with Arnold Quilt. He wanted to make money, they wanted to make revolution. No, they were just a small unconnected unit. You finished it."

"They had gotten into our computer system."

"No. Just Quilt had. He found the revolutionaries; they didn't find him."

"Where did he get the readout that called me recalcitrant, unstable, and idealistically confused?"

"From the computer bank, of course."

"I mean, who fed it in?" Remo asked.

"The computer had a list of humans it was supposed to analyze, and that was its own judgment. So that people could be continually measured against what they used to be. You'd be interested in knowing that ten years ago the computer declared you recalcitrant, unstable, and idealistically confused. You haven't changed at all."

"Nobody interviewed Chiun about me?"

"No. Is something wrong?"

"No," lied Remo. "You and I both know computers are big, dumb adding machines. I mean, you know me and, uh, it's just a silly readout. I'm not going to be offended by a computer readout."

"Get the clothes and the program, please. I'm going to rest. I feel awful."

"No drugs?"

"I refused them. I can't go under drugs, Remo. You know that."

"There's something that can help a bit. Not much, but a bit. Pain is really the body letting you know it's fighting to survive." Remo slipped his left hand between Smith's perspiration-wet white hair and the coarse fabric of the pillow, and where the spinal column met the skull, he applied light pressure.

"Now, breathe in slowly, like you're filling up your body with air. White air. Feel the white air come into you. Like the sun, it's light. Feel it? Feel it?"

"Yes. It's better now. Thank you."

"No dipwiddle computer can do that," Remo said.

He walked into the hallway, still resenting the computer that had insulted him steadily over the past ten years, and met a nurse outside the door who reminded him of a computer.

Her uniform was precisely starched and creased. She had a bland unresponsive face, and when she smiled, it was one of those plastic testimonials to overbite that you saw on television toothpaste commercials. Yes, she knew where Dr. Smith's clothes were. He had been asking for them before, which was peculiar because they were bloodied and shredded and his wallet and money were put by his bed to make him feel better. But he didn't seem satisfied. Almost as if he didn't care for the money or driver's license. Just wanted his clothes, no matter what shape they were in.

"Give him whatever he wants in the future," Remo said, flashing the sexy smile and exuding manhood around the nurse like a warm wet fog.

"Certainly," said the nurse unmoved. She flashed a small smile in return, sort of a hello acknowledgment to someone on the street you don't really want to talk to. But Remo did not really pay attention. His mind was on Smitty and the clothes and the computer that had insulted him.

The business office of Cape Cod General had the clothes in a plastic bag. And would the doctor like anything else?

"No, thank you," said Remo. Funny, the nurse outside Smith's room hadn't called him doctor.

In the stairwell, Remo searched the jacket pockets of the blood-moist clothes. His hands felt the stiff paper with the holes along the edge. The program. He took it out to check. There were the payroll figures with the little pencil marks that the late Arnold Quilt had put on them.

But there were no more white edges to the paper. The edges were red. The paper had been photocopied. Someone had gotten into the hospital and made a copy of that program. The sculpture that went boom had been no accident.

Remo took the stairs to Smith's room. He opened the door and was stunned. The bed, the support systems, all were gone. Only the black cord with a button to call the nurse hung uselessly from the wall. The room was empty.

"Nurse, what happened to my patient?" said

44

Remo to the plastic, smiling nurse whom he had asked to give Dr. Smith everything he wanted.

"He's been removed."

"Where is he?"

"Down the hall," said the nurse, pointing. Her hand moved funny, something most people wouldn't notice because they had not been trained to understand that even the bending of the finger involved the whole body. No part could move without the other parts adjusting. Yet this pointing hand just came up with its finger stuck out as if it weren't connected to a body, but a wall. Remo, senses sharp, noticed it. Perhaps the nurse had suffered some sort of nerve damage. That might explain why she had not responded to his overtures before.

Remo moved quickly down the hallway, but not so fast as to attract attention. A doctor running down a hall in the hospital would terrify any onlooker. Remo opened a door. There was a tent and the tubes going into a nose. But the face was wrinkled and surrounded by faded blonde hair. The patient was an old woman holding onto her last note of life. It was not Dr. Smith.

Down the hall behind him, the smiling plastic nurse pointed at Remo and said, "That's him."

Two overweight policemen nodded and waddled down the hall, their hands on their holsters. The nurse disappeared into a stairwell.

"You there, halt," said one officer. "Who are you?"

"I'm looking for a patient."

"So are we. Let's see your identification."

"I'm looking for a patient in the intensive care

45

unit. Middle-aged man. Have you seen a bed with support systems?" asked Remo.

"We want to know who you are."

Remo slipped through them and opened the next door. Another intensive care unit, but not Smith.

"You there, stop. What are you doing? We're officers. You've got to stop."

Remo checked the next ICU room. A child. Not Smith.

"You know you're avoiding arrest?"

"Later," said Remo. The next room was an old man. Then the empty room where Smith had been, and, finally, in the last room in the corridor, a middle-aged man. But not Smith.

"All right, buddy, you're under arrest," said the officer, out of breath from following Remo.

"Good," said Remo, not listening. "Fine." He looked for the nurse. The stairwell was empty. He looked for another nurse. None to be found. In an intensive care unit, to boot, not one nurse in sight. There was a gray metal swinging door that led to another corridor. More rooms. A maternity ward. No Smith.

"If you don't stop, I'm going to shoot," gasped the perspiring officer. His partner leaned against a wall, catching his breath at the other end of the corridor. Remo saw an elevator. Maybe the bed had been rolled into the elevator. He pressed the button. The elevator doors opened. Two green-coated men with green hats stood beside a table on wheels. The patient was covered by a sheet. Remo looked under the sheet while rubber-gloved hands tried to stop him. The head was bandaged. People yelled furious things at him while he made sure it wasn't Dr. Smith under the bandages.

The officer pointed the gun. Remo flicked on the safety catch of the .38 police special while the officer squeezed the trigger. Then Remo felt a fatty burden on his back. The officer was trying to wrestle him to the ground.

Remo put the officer outside the elevator doors and pressed "up." The men in green were on him. They went into the soft side padding of the elevator. The elevator was very slow. At each floor, Remo asked if anyone had seen an intensive care unit bed with a middle-aged man. No. Thank you. One of the green-coated men said he was a surgeon and demanded to be taken to the second floor. It was an emergency, and who was this lunatic, anyway?

"Shhhhhh," Remo said. "I'm busy."

When they reached the second floor, after checking the sixth, seventh, eighth, fourth and third, Remo let them out with their patient. Even the basement with the laundry room was bare. When Remo left through the parking lot, squad cars with brightly lit cherries on top were pulling in. Two patrolmen, guns drawn, ran into the hospital. Remo took their car and sped out into the town streets. The gear stuck in low. Other police cars skidded around and followed Remo.

He crashed through a barrier onto the beach. Churning sand, he drove the car into the surf, where he could slip out into the cool evening waters. The salt water enveloped his body, his legs and arms moving with the flow. The discarded doctor's robe floated, and he moved down to where the sand brushed his chest, his whole body snapping with the sharp rhythms of some large fish. In this way, he swam parallel to the shore and was seventy yards north when he surfaced and moved quietly to the darkened beach. Men fired plinking shots at the floating white coat back where he had left the car. Bathers on the beach saw the police firing, saw the coat floating and began shouting "Shark. Shark. Shark." By tomorrow the shark sighting would be covered by the press coast-to-coast, and the tourist business at Cape Cod would boom like it never had before.

"We're in trouble," said Remo, when he reached the small white cottage.

Chiun gestured that the situation was nothing. "I forgive you for being late. If I were not capable of forgiving, I could not endure you. It is my nature to forgive. But I warn you, no Persian king will be as forgiving. A Persian king will always demand the appearance of prompt service. But you know this."

"We're not going, Little Father," said Remo.

"Rest. You are wet from something," said Chiun.

"I said we're not going, Little Father. Smith is in trouble."

"And what trouble is that?"

"He's been injured. And kidnapped."

"Ah," said Chiun. "Then we must show that the House of Sinanju will not tolerate this. We will execute his bodyguards, and *then* we will leave for Persia."

"He didn't have bodyguards."

"Then why are you surprised by his misfortune? It was inevitable. It is quite clear he is mad and not even the House of Sinanju could save him. You recall that thus I have already written it in the

48

records. The archives know of the Mad Emperor Smith. There is no worry. No blame will attach to us."

"The organization is without a head."

"Beware," said Chiun. "You are an assassin, not an emperor. You have assassin's tools, not emperor's tools."

"I don't want Smitty's job."

"Then what concern is it of yours who is emperor?"

"It's the organization I care about. CURE."

"Why should you care about this organization?"

"Because I'm part of it, Little Father."

"Quite correct, and you have done your part, far beyond what anyone could expect." The long fingers rose, making a final point.

"It's not enough," said Remo. "If you want to go to Iran, go. I've got work here."

"The best thing a flower can do is bloom. It cannot plant seed or harvest seed." But Chiun's reasoning did not prevail. Every so often the lunacy of Western thought surfaced in this young man, and the Master of Sinanju decided he had better watch his pupil, lest in this insanity he hurt himself, squandering the wealth of knowledge that was the teaching of Sinanju.

4

Dr. Harold Smith had seen Remo go for the coat just before the nurse returned to the room.

"We are moving you," she had said, and he felt the bed glide to the door. The whole support system moved with him. Apparently it was a new bed, because the nurse moved it easily, as if it were a light wicker wheelchair. The overhead lights in the hallway looked like fogged moons because of the distortion of the oxygen tent's plastic. He heard elevator doors open and saw the ceiling of the elevator come over his bed. He felt the elevator lower.

"Am I going to be operated on, Nurse?"

"No," came the voice from behind his head. It was flat and mechanical.

Smith had felt fear before. The numb tension before a drop over France in World War II, when he was with the OSS. The silent scream of his mind in that Bucharest basement, when the NKVD passed overhead searching the houses, and Smith was with a professor torn between fleeing to the West and saving his life by turning in Smith. It was different fear then. Some things had still been in his control. And death could be quick.

Now he was helpless. His mind was trapped in a crippled, pained body to which any passerby had more access than himself. He could not move his left arm, and he knew that if he tried to raise his head he would pass out. His chest felt as if it had caught a pot of boiling lye, and his left eye throbbed.

He saw the elevator ceiling recede, and then he was in a basement of some sort. The nurse returned to the elevator, and he was alone.

It seemed like no more than a few minutes before she returned and wheeled him out into the cool spring-evening air that felt momentarily good on his body.

When he felt his body slip away as if he were floating under a sparkling lake, he heard cars screeching and police sirens. But that was far away. He was in a truck and the doors were shut behind him, because it was black all around him. Or was that because he could not see?

When the lights came, the very harsh lights that even shone into his bandaged eye like leaves of exploding orange, he heard no more cars. He smelled oil nearby and heard the sound of the sea coming up against rocks. His shoulder burned again.

"Well, Doctor Smith, I see that you are in pain." The voice sounded like the nurse. It was very flat. Smith could not see where it came from.

"Yes. Who are you? What am I doing here?"

51

"You are here to answer questions."

"I'll tell you anything," said Smith. "Why did you move me, though?"

"To get the truth, Wasp."

"What wouldn't I tell you, Nurse?"

"We will see. Now what nationality is Remo?"

"Who?"

"Remo. Your man. I know that Chiun, the aged one, is Korean. But what is Remo?"

"Remo who? Chiun who?"

The pain was sudden, like flesh being peeled by white-hot irons. Smith screamed.

"I'll tell you. Stop. Please, stop."

"Do you remember Remo and Chiun?"

"Yes, I know Remo and Chiun."

"Good. What nationality is Remo?"

"I don't know. I swear. He just sells us insurance at Folcroft Sanitarium."

The pain came again, gagging Smith with his own screams.

"All right, all right. We're CIA, Remo and I and Chiun. CIA. An intelligence center. We gather information on shipping and grain and . . ."

Someone seemed to be digging in Smith's chest with sandpaper tools. He passed out. Then the lights came again.

"All right." The flat voice. "Let us try again. Now I know you are protecting something, and I understand why. But it is not you or your organization I am after. I am after a more even chance with Remo and Chiun. All I want to do is survive. I cannot survive with your man in the world. I can offer you a replacement for him if you wish, one who is almost

as good, perhaps better. Myself. But you must coop-
erate."

"All right, but not in the chest again, please."

"You will find me very reasonable," the nurse
said.

"We don't know for sure what nationality Remo
is. He was an orphan."

"An orphan?"

"Yes."

"What is an orphan?"

"That's a person without parents."

"But a child cannot bear itself or rear itself. It
cannot even walk until after one year of age."

"He was raised by nuns in an orphanage."

"Where did he learn to do what he can do?"

"In the orphanage," Smith lied.

"Who in the orphanage taught him?"

"The nuns."

The pain was protracted this time.

"Chiun taught him," yelled Smith. "The Korean."

"And what of Chiun?"

"He is the Master of Sinanju," said Smith.

"They are teachers?"

"No."

"Good answer. What are they?"

"They are assassins," Smith said. "Sinanju is a
small village in Korea near China. It is the sun
source of all the martial arts. The masters, for centuries, have rented out their services to support the
people of the village."

"What services?"

"They are assassins. They sell their services.
Kings, pharaohs, czars, dictators, presidents,
chairmen, all hire them at times."

"Could I buy Chiun's services?"

"I don't know."

"Is Chiun creative?"

"I don't think so."

"What art does Chiun like?"

"We have in this country soap operas. Stories in the daytime on television. I take it you're not American, even if you don't speak with an accent," said Smith.

"Soap operas, you say?"

"Yes."

"And are they creative?"

"Not that I know of," said Smith honestly.

"But that is the strength of your species. Creativity. To be able to build from nothing, with new ideas."

"You must have had some good art in your country," said Smith. "Every country has some art that is good."

"You are trying to get a fix on me, are you not?"

"Yes," said Smith in fear that the pain would start again if he lied. "I am."

"Then I will trade. Almost everything between people is trading. I will tell you I created that statue in the town square that everyone disliked so much."

"I didn't dislike it," said Smith.

"You are not lying."

"How do you know that?" asked Smith.

"The voice changes during a lie. You may not notice it, but I do."

"Were you trained in an art like Sinanju?"

"No. I knew things that helped me teach myself other things. If I could be creative, I would fear nothing."

54

"Perhaps I can help," said Smith, and for the first time he began to suspect who ... or what ... the nurse was.

"Now you lie. What did you like about the sculpture?"

"It had a balance and a form that appealed to me."

"Others called it a lifeless imitation of Moore."

"I didn't think so," said Smith. "It had enough life for me."

"I was not sure you would stop to look at it. It was a low probability but worth trying. What was that printout in your pocket?"

"A payroll," said Smith.

"You are not lying, but your voice is changing somewhat."

"It is a payroll," said Smith.

"No matter that you lie. Could you tell Remo to kill himself and Chiun?"

"No," said Smith.

"It does not matter. You have helped me do the job, Wasp." The lights went off, and Smith looked out into blackness, filled in its center with a blue remnant that would disappear as his pupils adjusted. He breathed as deeply as he could and listened to the waves. He woke up again in a truck, and then, when the cool night air came over him again, he smelled hospital ether and felt the elevator going up, and when he woke up again, the sun was shining and there was the hall nurse.

"How are we feeling this morning, Dr. Smith?" she asked. "Your wife is here to see you. You gave us a fright last night. Where were you?"

"Don't you know?"

"Not at all," said the nurse.

"Well, I'll be," said Smith. He knew well the delusions of the wounded. Last night, he had been ready to swear that this nurse was an inhuman creature, a machine whose only purpose in life was to kill Remo and Chiun, and now here he was in his room, and here she was, and the room smelled clean and fresh-painted. Smith smiled and said again, "Well, I'll be ..."

"You most certainly will, Wasp," said the nurse, and the voice was flat and mechanical.

"Oh, my god," said Smith, and he lapsed back into unconsciousness from shock.

Meanwhile, Remo wrestled with a fear of his own. If Smith were captive somewhere, who was running the store? He asked that question of Chiun as they approached the gates of Folcroft Sanitarium. It was without any unusual number of guards, just a police pensioner at the gate, who said Remo needed a pass.

"Lather your armpits," said Remo.

"If you're going to be hostile, buddy, forget I spoke to you," said Folcroft's main gate protection, who went back to his small black and white television set. Chiun was missing his shows today, and he let Remo know.

"So who's watching the store?" asked Remo, as they strolled into the spaciously lawned interior of the old estate. Once before Remo had come back during an attempt to usurp control of the secret organization, and this time he noticed the protection was even less.

"I know I am not watching my beautiful daytime

56

dramas," said Chiun. "What other people are watching is not my concern."

"Funny how this place seems to change. The walls look so much less formidable."

"Doorknobs are always up in the air to children," said Chiun.

"You know," Remo said looking at the aged brick buildings, many heavy with years of ivy, "I'm not really sure what I'm looking for."

"But you think you will know it when you see it," Chiun said.

"Yeah. Right."

"You will never know it. Nothing is found that is not known before," Chiun said.

They strolled into a large old building that Remo remembered, his first gymnasium, where he had met Chiun and begun learning the ways of Sinanju. There were basketball hoops on the sides now, and mats and tumbling bars.

"I used to think guns and large numbers of men were powerful then," Remo said.

"You ate meat then, too," said Chiun.

"That was the hardest thing giving up. I used to dream of steaks. I remember how impressed I was when you cracked that two-by-four with your hand. I mean, just cracking a piece of wood and I thought it was wonderful. You know, I never understood half the things you told me then."

"Then?" said Chiun, cackling. "Then?"

"Sure, then."

"Which explains why we wander around here uselessly, not even knowing what we look for. I tell you, Remo, you have caused me great disturbance in my peace."

"What are you worried for?" asked Remo. An exercise class, apparently of employees, filled the far end of the gym. They puffed back and forth across the wooden floor two times, then stretched their muscles in exercises that Remo recognized as contrary, that is, one exercise worked against another so that people strained instead of increasing in power.

"Was I that bad, Little Father?"

"Worse," said Chiun. "You were a drinker of alcohol, an eater of meat, violent in your movements, and contemptuous and venal in your character."

"Yeah. What a change."

"Yes. You no longer drink alcohol or eat meat."

Walking to Smith's office overlooking Long Island Sound, Remo told Chiun of the incident at the hospital.

"What of that nurse?" asked Chiun. "Did she remind you of anyone you have met before?"

"No."

"Were you concentrating when you met her?"

Remo paused. "No. I was thinking of something the computer said."

"Well, we shall see," said Chiun.

"See what?"

"I do not know. But we *will* know. We will know because we will not seek. We will let whatever looks for us find us."

"That's a minor problem, Little Father. The whole organization may be going under."

"Wrong," said Chiun. "Your problem is your life. Your organization's problem is your organization's problem. If it is not to survive, then it is not to survive. Have you heard of the Aztec kings? Where are they now? Where are the czars? Where are the pharaohs? They are not. The House of Sinanju survives because it does not wallow in foreign trivia."

"I've got a job, Little Father."

The receptionist in Smith's office said he was not in that day.

"Any calls for him?" asked Remo.

"With all due respect, sir, that's none of your business. He is in a hospital in Cape Cod. You might try telephoning him. He told me there were certain items he would be able to handle by phone, and if your..."

"When did you speak to him?" interrupted Remo.

"This morning."

"What?"

"Forgive him, child," said Chiun. "He does not know what he is doing."

Remo phoned the hospital. It was true. There had been an incident the night before, but Cape Cod General could not be held responsible, and the patient wanted no notoriety.

Remo and Chiun reached the hospital by late afternoon. Remo explained to Chiun that he couldn't exactly go in. He might be recognized. He was, well, sort of running from the police yesterday.

"Why were you running from the police? Are you trying to be a thief now, as well as an emperor?"

"I can't explain," said Remo. They waited until nightfall and entered through an alley basement door and walked up the stairs to Smith's room.

The same nurse was on duty.

"I want to talk to you," said Remo.

"Doctor Smith will see you now," she said.

"Hold," said Chiun. "Do not go farther, Remo. Get away from that nurse."

"The old one remembers me," said the nurse. "Breasts and makeup do not fool the old man, do they?"

"What's going on?" said Remo.

"If you want to see Doctor Smith, enter," said the nurse.

"Remo, is that you?" came Smith's voice from the room.

"I'm going in," said Remo, but he felt the long fingers of Chiun on his back. He tried to bend away from them, but they kept with him, and he skidded on the slippery floor wax.

He saw the nurse make a move toward them, but then Chiun was up, circling in his deceptive slow movements, making almost imperceptible feints with the long fingers. The nurse, too, circled. Remo noticed that she limped.

"Gracious," she said in the flat mechanical voice. "I remember exactly. I think you have me, gook."

In Korean, Chiun ordered Remo to join in. For a nurse? The Master of Sinanju needed help with a nurse?

Remo moved into Chiun's circular pattern so that he was opposite the Master, with the nurse in the center.

"Maybe you can help me with a paraplegic sometime, Little Father," said Remo.

"Do not joke. This one moves backwards equal with forwards and does all things with balance beyond men."

"I was pretty well programmed that way," said the nurse. "But I still doubt that I could duplicate some of your moves."

"Who are you?" said Remo.

"What is a better question," said Chiun, and in Korean, he ordered Remo to hold.

The nurse's head spun around like the turret on a tank. She looked at Remo, smiling, her chin directly above her backbone.

"Oh," said Remo.

"I see you remember," said the nurse. "I wouldn't attack right now if I were you, human. It would result in the destruction of Smith. Immediately."

"Remo," called Smith. "Who's out there?"

"Do not move, oh, Emperor. We are saving your life," said Chiun.

"There's somebody after you," said Smith weakly. "I think it's Mr. Gordons."

"You're a great help," mumbled Remo.

"I see we are at an impasse, gook and orphan," said the nurse.

"What's happening?" yelled Smith as loudly as his strength let him.

"Take two aspirin and call me in the morning," Remo yelled back.

"There was a high probability that you should enter the room with Smith. Why didn't you?"

"Do not tell him, Remo," said Chiun.

"Let's finish the old business now," said Remo.

"No," Chiun said.

"I see you are the better thinker, gook," the nurse said.

"One does not need special wisdom to see that," Chiun said. "What do you want?"

"Your destruction," said the nurse.

"Why?" said Chiun.

"Because while you live you are a danger to me."

"We can share the earth."

"I am not here to share the earth. I am here to survive," said the nurse. "You and your pale whelp are the one force I must destroy."

As the nurse spoke, another nurse passed them in the hall, nodded toward the nurse between Remo and Chiun and entered Smith's room.

Remo watched her go in. A moment later she came out. She walked away down the hall.

"See, you may go in now," the first nurse said in that flat voice. "It is safe now."

"Remo, stay away from that door," said Chiun. "Why do you wish to destroy us?" he asked the nurse.

"Because you two represent a force that has been continuing for centuries and centuries. Is that not right, gook?"

"Correct," said Chiun.

"Then there is no reason that it might not be many centuries more. I have determined that I could outlast any country just by disappearing for a while, until it is no longer the country it was. But you humans of Sinanju stay around forever. Better we meet now, rather than I unexpectedly meet one of your descendants centuries from now."

"Blow it out your transistors," Remo said and moved into a two-line attack that could converge the maximum force upon the target. He needed only a piece of this thing to rip it apart. A normal blow to the heart or brain was useless. The motor responses could be anywhere. The last time they were in the creature's stomach; now they could be under the nurse's hat. Inside the white shoes.

"No," said Chiun to Remo. "Smith will die. Stop."

"He knows," said the nurse.

"What's going on out there?" yelled Smith.

"What have you done, thing?" said Chiun.

"That is for you to find out. I am leaving, but remember, I will destroy you. Goodbye."

"Goodbye, thing, and let me tell you this. All that was made by man disappears. But man continues."

"I'm a new generation of thing, gook."

Remo watched, puzzled, as the nurse walked smoothly to an exit door.

"It is good that you have learned to listen," Chiun said.

"What's going on?" asked Remo.

"First, how did it hurt Emperor Smith to begin with?"

"Exploding sculpture," said Remo.

"Explosion," said Chiun. He went to the entrance of Smith's room and called in:

"What is new in the room you are in?"

"Nothing," said Smith. "What's going on?"

"I smell something," said Chiun.

"Just some fresh paint."

"The whole room is painted?"

"Yes," said Smith.

"And paint covers things," Chiun said.

"What's going on?" asked Smith.

"Nothing to fear. Just get well and do not leave your sickness room until we tell you it is safe."

63

"Come here and tell me," said Smith. "Why are we yelling at each other like this?"

"That, oh, Emperor, is impossible," said Chiun. "You are in a trap. And I would imagine that that thing without imagination prepared a device similar to the one he used before."

"I don't see any statue," Smith said.

"The walls, the room. That is the bomb. And I am sure should we have entered before, both you and your faithful servants would be injured, probably unto death."

"My God, what can we do?" Smith asked.

"Get well and do not leave your room, for I fear your leaving will set off this device in some way. I do not know your modern methods. But of this I am sure. The paint covers death on four sides."

"The ceiling is freshly painted too," said Smith.

"Five sides," said Chiun.

"I could get men here to dismantle it," said Smith.

"How do you know they would not set it off? Just get well. When the time comes for you to leave your room I shall show you how."

"What are you going to do?"

"Hopefully save you by doing what we do best, oh, gracious Emperor," said Chiun.

"Speedy recovery, Smitty," said Remo. "Don't let it worry you that you're sleeping in the middle of a bomb."

And Chiun noted that if they had left for the riches of Persia, Smith might not have found himself in the center of a boom boom.

"That's a bomb," said Remo.

"And you would have walked into it," said Chiun.

"How did I know we were dealing with Mr. Gordons?" Remo said. "I was hoping he was in a junkyard someplace, after the last time." And going down the steps, not knowing even what to look for, Remo felt an old, forgotten sensation. He was afraid.

5

Dr. Robert Caldwell was not an alcoholic. Could an alcoholic walk away from a half-filled glass of scotch down at Mitro's? Could an alcoholic go on the wagon three or four days in a row? Could an alcoholic have gone through medical school?

Could an alcoholic have prepared the four brains in trays with labels the way Dr. Caldwell had? He was not an alcoholic. The hospital administration had been against him. It would drive anyone to drink.

If he were an alcoholic he wouldn't have been able to close a deal for a full year's income just to explain certain things to that man. And that man had come to him. Had heard about him. Dr. Robert Caldwell was still a better neurosurgeon dead drunk than most of the knife pushers were sober. The dictum against surgeons drinking had been set up when America was still in the Victorian age. Many times Dr. Caldwell had operated better with a couple of settling drinks in him than he did shaky sober. But how could you tell that to a teatotaling hospital administration? They were hypocrites. And his own colleagues had turned on him, that young intern pushing him out of the operating room. Physically.

Dr. Caldwell entered the loft building just off Houston Street in New York City. It wasn't a hospital, but it didn't have to be. The man was buying his wisdom. His experience. His insight. He wasn't buying an operation.

If he were getting an operation, that would be different. But for this, the loft would do. It didn't have to be sanitary. The four brains certainly weren't going to mind a little dust. They had been torn out of their skulls so roughly you couldn't tell the frontal cerebro-corticopontal tract from the sensory tract. They were almost mush anyhow. So he had put them in trays and covered them with bags. He had meant to store them in the refrigerator. But it wouldn't have mattered. So he forgot to store them exactly as he had planned. So what? They were mush anyhow, and when he saw the first light coming through the dusty loft windows he realized he had—well, anyone could have done it—slept on them. But he got them into the refrigerator right then ... Laymen didn't know how indestructible a brain could be. He just wouldn't tell the man. That's all.

Dr. Caldwell was grateful he had a couple of drinks in him. Going up the steps was such a burden. If he hadn't had a couple of drinks, he might not have bothered at all. But here he was, at the top of the steps, at the door in one long run. And feeling good. He searched for the key, and while doing so, leaned against the door. It was open.

He turned on the light switch by pulling the string beside the door, and three unshaded bulbs hanging from the ceiling cast an eyeblinking yellow light throughout the loft. There were the refrigerator, the display table and the textbooks. It was all set for tonight. He shut the door behind him and went to the refrigerator. There were four trays. Filling each was a gray whitish mass, like a deflated beach ball with knurls. Each glistened under the harsh yellow light from above as he carried each tray to a table by the wall. The client had labeled each one, and Dr. Caldwell would have to replace the labels with his own. Not that it mattered. What difference was there between a singer's brain and a painter's brain and a sculptor's brain and a dancer's brain?

He would do it after he had a drink. After all, hadn't he left a half-glass of scotch down at Mitro's? In the small room with the toilet were three cardboard cases of rye whiskey.

If Dr. Caldwell were an alcoholic, he wouldn't have left these bottles and gone to Mitro's. He just would have stayed here in the loft with the booze and drunk himself into a stupor. But he had gone to Mitro's and drunk at the bar like any other serious drinker and had left a half-glass there.

He got a glass from the refrigerator and washed it out in the giant tubs right near the refrigerator. An alcoholic would have drunk right from the bottle.

He was feeling rather good when his client arrived. The client had a nurse's uniform folded under his arm. Dr. Caldwell offered him a drink, but the client refused. He was a stiff sort of man in his early thirties, with very blue eyes and incredibly neat brown hair.

"Well, glad you could make it, Mr. Gordons," said Dr. Caldwell. "You know there's a famous gin named after you. Heh, heh."

"Incorrect," said Mr. Gordons. "I was named after the gin. We all were. But my system worked."

"Well, some parents do irreparable damage."

"You are all my parents. All the science of man is my parents."

"A noble sentiment," said Dr. Caldwell. "Would you care for a drink?"

"No. I want what I paid you for."

"And paid well, too," said Caldwell, hoisting his glass. "Paid well. A toast to your generosity, sir. To Mr. Gordons."

"Have you done it?"

"Basically, I've got the total orientation, but I could use some specific parameters."

"In what direction?"

"Exactly what it is you want from the brains."

"I told you the last time," said Dr. Gordons.

"But you also said, and I remember well, that this might not be necessary. I remember that," said Dr. Caldwell. He freshened his drink a bit. If there was one thing he hated it was people who changed their minds. Hated. You needed a drink to deal with those kind of people.

"What I said was that I was going to do something that would make your services less crucial if

69

what I was going to do succeeded, juicehead. It did not succeed. It failed."

"Jesus. Have a drink. I know what you mean. This will take the bite out of it."

"No, thank you. Have you done it?"

"I don't think you were all that clear last time," said Dr. Caldwell. He was getting tired of standing. Didn't Mr. Gordons ever get tired? Dr. Caldwell sat down on the edge of the table and leaned on his left hand. Whoops. One of the brains. It was all right. No damage. He assured Mr. Gordons that brains were a lot tougher than laymen thought. Sticky things though, weren't they?

"I gave you four brains, severed at the medula. The occipital lobe, the parietal lobe, the temporal lobe, and the front lobes were all undamaged."

"Right," said Dr. Caldwell. He needed a medical lecture from this clown like he needed an asphalt enema.

"I was especially careful of the occipital lobe, which we do know is the area of elaboration of thought."

"Good," said Dr. Caldwell. "Very good. You pronounce medical terms very well. Sure you didn't study medicine?"

"Medicine was fed into me."

"Intravenously?"

"No, medical knowledge. Garbage in, garbage out."

"Heh, heh, you sound like a computer."

"In a way. But not as viable as I should like."

"Don't we all feel that way?" said Dr. Caldwell. He drank to that.

"Now, have you isolated that area of the brain

70

which has the greatest creativity? What we will do once we isolate this area is transform the weak electro-chemical signals of the body to electronic signals that I can use. We would need living people for that."

"Brilliant," said Dr. Caldwell. "I toast your genius."

"Have you done it?"

"No," said Dr. Caldwell.

"Why not?"

"I think we're approaching this unscientifically."

"I am open to your suggestions."

"Let's discuss it over a drink at Mitro's."

"I need no drink, and you have one."

"All right. I'll be frank. I took this case hoping I would be able to help you. But you haven't helped me."

"In what way?" asked Mr. Gordons.

"I need more information. You haven't been honest with me."

"I am incapable of being dishonest under normal circumstances."

"On that, sir, I will say you need a psychiatrist. A psychiatrist. It is humanly impossible to be honest all the time. Impossible. Thank you for coming, but I think your case is hopeless, and frankly, I need a good drink now more than I need an incurable patient. I always get the hopeless ones. When they're terminal, give 'em to old Caldwell. No wonder I have to drink. Do you know how many people I've had to tell that their loved ones did not survive operations?"

"No."

"Plenty. I figured out that I, more than any doc-

tor in the hospital, had to inform more families of
the deaths of their loved ones than anyone else. Any
other doctor. Even those cancer freaks. You know
why?"

"Possibly."

"I'll tell you why. I got the shit patients. I'd get
tumors that weren't quite what they looked like on
X-rays. I'd get brain structure that, while it looked
normal, wasn't really all that normal, and all the
while, with these really fucked-up brains, nurses be-
traying me with vicious little lies about drunken-
ness. Vicious. That was all I needed to top off the
worst patient list in the hospital. Send the disasters
to Caldwell. And now I've got another one. You."

"I said I was incapable under most circumstances
of being dishonest. In my case this is not a mental
illness but a scientific fact. It takes creativity to be
a truly good liar. I seek creativity."

"You want to be creative," said Dr. Caldwell,
filling his glass angrily. Who wouldn't drink, with
these dumdums all around? "You want to be creative, you go to Hollywood. You want the best brain
surgeon ever held a scalpel, you come to me. Now
what the fuck do you want from me?"

"I thought you would isolate that area of the
brain that provides creativity."

"It's in the occipital lobe. And no, you can't transform creative waves. Just impulses which aren't
creativity." Dr. Caldwell weaved from the table,
with the rye bottle firmly in his left hand, the glass
in his right.

"You want brilliant brain surgery? Here I am.
But don't come to me with creativity nonsense. I'm
a brain surgeon." There was something slippery on

72

the floor, and Dr. Caldwell lost his balance. Very close to the wooden floor now, he searched for what he had slipped on. Couldn't find it. He got to his feet again, rather easily. He was being helped up by Mr. Gordons. Strong sonuvabitch, but weren't the insane always strong?

Why was it he always got the weirdos? This one even started on the story of his life. Mr. Gordons was born two years ago. Two years ago? Right. Okay. I'll drink to that. A two-year-old who looked like he was in his mid-thirties and hoisted brilliant brain surgeons around as if they were feathers.

Wasn't born exactly. Well, that was nice. Maybe he was immaculately conceived? No, he wasn't. Not in that sense although his first environment was incredibly free of dust and germs. He was one of a generation of space products. Vehicles created to survive in outer space.

Mr. Gordons was an android. He was the best of the space machines. His inventor was a brilliant scientist but she found herself unable to design a truly creative machine, one that could think for itself in unforeseen situations. She did the best she could. She invented Mr. Gordons who was a survival machine. While he could not be creative, he could find ways to survive. He could change his appearance, his functions. Anything to survive.

His inventor had had a drinking problem also. She named all her space inventions for brands of alcohol. Hence Mr. Gordons. Sometimes he used Mr. Regal. But that was unimportant. At one point, it became a verified fact that to stay at the laboratory where he had been created would mean destruction, and so he left.

73

He had no great problems except for two humans who would ultimately destroy him, if he did not destroy them. For this, Mr. Gordons needed access to creativity. Did Dr. Caldwell understand?

"What do you mean 'drinking problem also'?"

"You are an alcoholic."

"What do you know? You're a machine anyhow. Hey, don't bother me. You want some Hollywood agent. Not me."

And then something peculiar happened. Along with the brains, Dr. Caldwell found himself shut inside the refrigerator. And it was cold. But he didn't mind. He had his bottle, and besides, he felt sleepy.

Very sleepy.

6

Remo stretched his arms slowly, reaching farther and farther. He pushed his heels out farther and farther. He let the air come into his lungs more and more, and then, when he was at the fullest capacity, he held, suspended like a white light in an eternity of darkness. He felt beyond the mat on which he lay face downward, beyond the motel room in Burwell, Nebraska. He was one with the original light, light of life, force in voice, one.

If a passerby could have looked into the motel room, he would have seen a man lying on a mat on the floor with his arms and legs outstretched, not even stretched beyond normal. He would have seen the figure lying very still. And he would have passed on and missed the uniqueness of the exercise.

For Remo was this way nearly half an hour, and his heartbeat had slowed close to death. Even his blood pumped more lightly, the heart at the very shallow edge of stopping.

The light filled and was him. And then he let it go. Slowly. First from his fingers, then from his toes, up his limbs, the light returning quietly to the universe, and then it left his shoulders and his head and his heart. With a snapping motion, the flat form was on its feet, and Remo was breathing normally.

Chiun was catching up on his daytime dramas. A taping device which had been provided by CURE picked up those shows which ran simultaneously so that Chiun could watch the soap operas for six hours straight, though lately he complained about their filth and violence. He was now seeing the taped reruns of the shows he had missed on the day they had gone to Folcroft. He began at dawn, and at 11 A.M. he would switch to the current shows.

"Disgusting," said Chiun as Varna Haltington made a lewd suggestion to Dr. Bruce Andrews, whom she knew to be married to Alice Freemantle, her own niece, who had been raped by Damien Plester, an ex-minister of the Universal Realism Church, and who was now contemplating an abortion. According to Remo's recollection, Alice had been contemplating this abortion since the previous March, and the kid should have been born by now, a normal fourteen-month full-term infant, weighing somewhere between forty and fifty pounds.

"Vice. Disgusting. Degeneracy," said Chiun as yesterday's commercials came on.

"Then why don't you stop watching them, Little Father?"

"Because I trusted you a long time ago when you promised to keep such filth out of my daytime dramas and I continue to wait, without real hope, for you to live up to your promise."

"Hold on. I never . . ." But Remo stopped. He had exactly forty-four seconds to speak to Chiun, and he preferred to discuss the collapse of the organization, Smith's trap, whether Remo and Chiun had any chance, and what they should do about it.

"Why are we in Burwell, Nebraska?" Remo asked.

"We are attacking that thing."

"How are we attacking in Burwell, Nebraska. Is he here?"

"Of course not. That is why we are here."

"Don't you think we should go where he is?"

"Where is he?" asked Chiun.

"I don't know."

"Then how can we go there?" asked Chiun.

Varna Haltington returned to the screen, asking two things from Dr. Andrews. His body and the emotional condition of his wife, Alice, and would she have an abortion? They discussed Alice's abortion sympathetically until Varna put her hands on Dr. Andrews' shoulders signifying sex and the end of the episode.

"So how are we attacking?" Remo asked.

"Were you not at the hospital? Did you not hear?"

"Yeah, I heard. We called him dirty names and he called us dirty names."

"You are given maps and you see nothing," said Chiun. "It is he who fears time, not us. He must attack."

"That gives him the initiative."

"No, it does not," Chiun said.

"Why not?"

"Because he does not know where we are."

"So?" asked Remo.

"So he must find us."

"I don't think he can definitely do that."

"Exactly. So he must do things to attract us. And that will let us know where he is."

"And then we walk into another one of his traps," said Remo and waited through another soap opera. This time Katherine made a lewd suggestion to Dr. Drake Marlen, whom she knew to be married to Nancy Whitcomb, who had not been raped but was thinking about an abortion anyway, because she was in love with her psychiatrist.

"Why," said Remo when the commercial came on, "should he fear time and not us? I mean, metal and transistors outlast flesh."

"If you had been listening in the hospital, you would have heard me put the thought into his mind which he accepted because it was true."

"I didn't hear any thought," said Remo.

"Man outlasts everything he makes."

"That's not true. Just look at tombstones," said Remo.

"Look at them," Chiun said. "Show me the tombstones of the Scythians, the ancient markers of the Celtic tribes. All are gone, and yet the Persians survive and the Irish live fresh as a newborn baby's smile."

"The pyramids."

"Look at them in decay. And look at the Egyptians. Look too at the fragment of a great temple, the wailing wall of the Jews. And look at the new Israelis. No, man renews himself, and his things do not. The thing understood. He knew that the House of Sinanju passed on from one master to another master and would be here strong and new and alive when his tinkerings had begun to rust. It is he who must destroy us now, not we who must destroy him."

"Why didn't he take me in the hospital? When he was disguised as a nurse and could have had the jump on me?"

"He probably thought you were conscious. Which proves that even gadgets can make mistakes. Also he may fear what one of us will do if the other is killed. He seems to want to dispatch us both at once. Hence the bomb in Smith's room."

"That's another problem. Smitty."

"There are other emperors in the world."

"I happen to have loyalty to this one."

"The House of Sinanju is famous for its loyalty. Loyalty is one thing, but stupidity another. We are unique. Emperors are many. We owe many loyalties and the first is to Sinanju, although this you have not yet understood, and you should, of all people, because someday you will be the Master of Sinanju."

"We've got to do something for Smitty," Remo insisted.

"If we had gone to Persia, Smith would be uninjured. For any emperor, the best thing one can do is serve him in his capacity and no more."

"I don't buy that. Even though he's not in his office playing with his computer, he's still the boss. Mine and yours."

"Yours perhaps," said Chiun. "Not mine. You may be an employee but I am an independent contractor." He raised a hand. "But we will save Smith."

"How?"

"You saw the nurse, the human nurse, who walked into his room without offsetting the bomb?"

"Setting off. Yes, I saw her."

"The bomb is for us. For you and me. We will protect Smith by staying away from him and not offsetting the bomb."

"Setting off," said Remo, but Chiun was not listening. He had turned back to the television set and Remo had to sit through the current day's "As the Planet Revolves" and "The Wrought and the Rampant" before he could get an answer to another nagging problem.

"What trap do you think Gordons will use against us?" Remo said.

"The trap we tell him to," said Chiun and would talk no more of the subject because to continue to pour water over a wet stone did not make it any wetter.

In the afternoon, Remo phoned Smith from a pay phone in a nearby roadhouse.

The jukebox was playing something that sounded like a teenager's whine set to drums. Several motorcyclists in black jackets, with hair that looked as if it had been combed with tree roots from a mangrove swamp, drank beer and threatened people. The bartender attempted to preserve his manhood by scrupulously not noticing. If he were aware, he would have to do something about it. He didn't want to try.

Remo got Smith and found out he was feeling better, "considering."

"They're taking the bandages off the left eye by the end of the week, and I've stabilized. They say I should be able to try to walk next week."

"Don't," said Remo.

"I know that," said Smith. "Do you have any good leads. You know I can't get anything going from a hospital bed with open lines. I'm even afraid to install secure lines. Who knows what will set the thing off?"

"Yeah," said Remo.

"Leads?" asked Smith again.

"Yeah. We're ... uh, moving on a plan."

"Good," said Smith. "If it weren't for you, I'd probably have given up."

"Hang in there, Smitty," said Remo, feeling very small.

"Same to you, Remo."

Remo hung up and ordered a glass of spring water from the bartender. A motorcyclist with ape-hairy arms and an old German helmet painted with a swastika offered Remo something stronger.

"I don't drink," Remo said. "Drink, smoke, eat meat or entertain ambivalent or hostile thoughts."

"What do you do, faggo?" said the cyclist, laughing. He turned to his friends, who laughed with him. They had a live one. The back of the jacket said in pink and white paint: "Rat Skulls."

"I'm a hand surgeon," said Remo.

"Yeah? What's a hand surgeon?"

"I improve faces with my hand."

"Yeah? Improve mine, faggo, heh, heh."

"Oh, thank you for the invitation," said Remo, leaving the bar to stand close to the table with the rest of the Rat Skulls.

"Now, gentlemen, I will show you how I can catch a nose in my hands," said Remo.

"That's a shitty kid's trick," said one of the Rat Skulls. "You pass your hand over a kid's face and stick your thumb between your fingers and say, hey, look kid, I got your nose."

"Let's let him do it," said the Rat Skull, lumbering over from the bar. "Go ahead. Do it, faggo, and then I'll show you my chain surgery." He looked down at Remo and clanked a large towing chain.

The others played with their beer and laughed.

"C'mon, fellas," said the bartender.

"You say something?" asked the Rat Skull with the chain.

"I'm saying, only, you know, this is a bar, and . . ."

"He started it," said the Rat Skull with the chain, nodding to Remo.

"Well, sure, okay," said the bartender. "I know you guys have to protect yourselves."

"Yeah," said the Rat Skulls in unison.

"Are you ready?" Remo asked pleasantly.

"Yeah. Yeah. Ready," said the Rat Skulls.

"No vomitty, vomitty," said Remo. "It can be bloody."

"We don't upchuck," said a Rat Skull.

"Good. Because there's a penalty if you get sick. You lose your nose, too."

"Go ahead," said the Rat Skull with the chain, and he chuckled.

"Here comes the handsy wandsy," said Remo, fluttering his fingers. The hand started slow, like the backswing of a golfclub, but when it came down it looked as if it were yanked on the end of a whip.

Two fingers separated and Remo's hand closed on the face, and the two fingers joined together again, and there was a snap as if the whip had been cracked. The Rat Skull with the chain felt a sharp tug as if a baby tooth had been pulled. From the middle of his face. His breathing was suddenly funny also. Like he was drawing breath directly into his head. But it was moister than breath. He stood there dumbly with a big red splash in the middle of his face and two holes in the middle of the red splash and it stung.

"Got your nosey wosey," said Remo coyly and he showed the sitting Rat Skulls his right hand. Protruding from two fingers might have been a thumb. If thumbs had nostrils.

Remo opened his hand and dropped the lump of flesh into a Rat Skull's beer which turned a pinkish gold.

"No uppy chuck," said Remo.

"Oh, Jeez," said the Rat Skull with a nose in his beer. And one might have thought they would take this harshly and not in the spirit of fun and games. But Remo prevailed upon them all. They certainly wanted no hostilities. Especially after Remo informed them he was also a genital surgeon.

They all agreed it was only fun and games.

"Drink your beer," said Remo, and the Rat Skull with the pink beer passed out.

On the short drive back to the motel in the rented car, Remo listened to a radio panel discussion on prison reform. One woman complained about the violence of the law.

"Violence by the law only encourages more

disorders," she said. She did not mention that as the police used their guns less and less, more and more people stayed prisoners in their homes from fear of those outside the law who did use violence. Remo thought of the Rat Skulls back at the roadhouse and how, if he could not have defended himself extraordinarily well, he might have been just another victim.

It did not surprise Remo to hear that the woman lived in a very expensive high rise apartment in Chicago. She was being magnanimous with the lives of those people who could not afford doormen.

The law was becoming less efficient in fighting street crime, the punishments were becoming lighter, and therefore street crime rose. It was not complicated. Only the solutions were complicated. Like this woman on the radio who thought that all the government had to do was to transform the nature of the human animal. To do that, she called for abolishing prisons.

"They don't cure anybody anyway. The criminal comes out more hardened than before." If anybody had any further ideas on the subject, she would be interested in hearing them. They could write her.

At her summer place on the outskirts of Manitoba.

7

Wanda Reidel had the package, so why was Summit Studios acting like assholes? She had an Academy Award director, an Academy Award writer, and the one actor who could make it all go, and did Summit want to pass up another *Godfather*? Another *Sting*? Was that the kind of business Summit was in, because if it was in that kind of business, she wasn't forgetting that they had some very important shareholders who were already miffed about the last deal they blew, and crowns did not rest easily on the heads of studio chiefs.

"Threatening? Who's threatening?" said Wanda. Her secretary leaned lovingly over her puffy pale body with the red lips, rearranging the gray-blonde hair that Wanda's hairdresser assured her was "Wanda."

"It's you, precious loved one," he had said. The

hair looked like Hollywood-stucco. Wanda Reidel or Ms. Reidel or "the Octopussy," as she was known in Hollywood, covered herself in original print muu-muus and a treasury of jewels, which gave the impression of a geodesic dome draped in Appalachian neon and spangled with shiny green-and-white rocks. These rocks looked very much like costume jewelry popular in the Bronx where Wanda was raised.

When the Octopussy had her first million-dollar month, she had a Rome jeweler construct the jewelry to her specifications. Two of his artisans quit. But that was more than made up for by his new clients. If you wanted to be in with Wanda, you bought your jewels at her favorite store in Rome.

One actress even ordered a $20,000 brooch, with this instruction: "Make it Wanda-style schlock."

In Hollywood, it was called "Wandaful Jewelry." The artisans who had crafted universal elegance for the Windsors, Rothschilds and Krupps, using the genius of Cellini, now followed closely what was selling in Woolworth's off the Grand Concourse on Fordham Road.

"I'm not threatening," said Wanda. "I don't threaten. I make money magic. If your shareholders get on your ass because you don't make money for them, it's not my fault."

"Wanda, darling," said Del Stacy, who also had a marine nickname in Hollywood—the Crustacean—"you could get away with this at the beginning of your career a long time ago, but not now."

"What's a long time ago?" Wanda asked.

"Last Thursday. You're slipping, precious."

"Hah," said Wanda, with a bubbly little chuckle.

"Kiss, kiss." But when she put down the phone, the sunshine left her face for a dark, brooding storm.

"Get the fuck out of here, cunt," she said to her secretary.

"Yes, precious," said the secretary.

When the secretary had backed out in the bowing posture that the Octopussy required, Wanda drummed her green fingernails with the inset cameos of the Taj Mahal, onto the mother of pearl desktop. A former studio vice president had once suggested that the desktop looked like formica in a wetback kitchen. He was now selling tractor supplies in Burbank.

She glanced out her pink-tinted windows at Sunset Boulevard. The little bastard at Summit was right. She was slipping. Not a great big slip, but what more did you need to become Lash Larue or Mack Sennett in a town where breakfast was yesterday?

The Summit deal had to go through. It was really a very good deal. A perfect package. Everyone would make money. An Academy Award director, an Academy Award writer, and the one actor who could make it all go.

Unfortunately the writer was under contract to another agent, and the director wasn't talking to her. A peculiar sort of sickie who nurtured unreasonable grudges, he, childlike, had become fixated with an impossible promise and, childlike, wouldn't let go of it or even slightly forget that he didn't get the toy that was precisely promised. Marlon Brando. Marlon Brando. Marlon Brando. The name got stuck in his mouth like a broken record. Marlon Brando.

He couldn't understand Brando was booked. Couldn't, in any mature manner, see that one actor was impossible and therefore, like a grownup, you used what was possible. Brando was booked, so you used Biff Ballon.

"What's the difference?" Wanda had asked. "Biff can play the grandfather. You dye his beautiful blond hair. You cover up his beautiful muscles with padding. Let me tell you, it would be easier to get Biff made up for the grandfather part than it would be to get Marlon physically in shape for *Racket Lover*. I'd like to see Marlon swing from a burning building with a tommy gun in one hand and a knife in his teeth without messing his hair."

But juvenile obstinacy was juvenile obstinacy. So the director wouldn't talk to her, and the writer didn't talk to anybody unless his own agent said so.

So when Wanda Reidel had told Summit Pictures that she had the writer and the director and the actor, she was not quite accurate. She had the actor. Biff Ballon.

She needed something. She needed the big deal. That crustacean bastard was joking and not joking when he said she was through. She needed that deal, and she needed it by cocktail hour, or supper at the latest, or she would be washed up and tomorrow's breakfast would see her retired.

"Danish," she screamed. "I want a Danish."

The secretary scurried in.

"Strawberry Danish," yelled Wanda Reidel.

"But loved one, you know how angry you'll be after you've eaten."

"Strawberry Danish. I won't be angry. Give it to me."

"But you know after you've eaten it, you'll hate the world."

"I already hate the world. I'll love the world with a Danish."

"But loved one, your diet."

"I want the Strawberry Danish." The voice of the Octopussy was heard in the office like the atmosphere of a cold, haunting, unused dark room that one not only did not enter but pretended did not exist. To this voice, secretaries did not argue.

"Six Strawberry Danish," corrected Wanda Reidel and six arrived soon after, carried by a white-coated counterboy with a nameplate.

"Heublein," said the secretary to the boy, reading his nameplate. "Just leave the Danish here."

"This is for the great Wanda Reidel, correct?" the boy asked.

"Yes, yes, and she doesn't want to be disturbed," said the secretary.

"I just wanted to see her. I have difficulty telling people from their pictures. People look different from their pictures."

"Just leave the Danish," said the secretary, but the delivery boy was already through the next door in Wanda Reidel's office.

"Ms. Reidel," said the delivery boy, "I can do wonders for you. You have access to more creativity than anyone else. I have read that in many places. You would be surprised at what I can do for you."

"That's great," said Wanda. "This is such Hollywood. Del Stacey of Summit who has the money I need won't spring it, and I get the backing of a luncheonette employee."

89

"Leave, please," said the secretary, bustling into the room. "Ms. Reidel hates the little people."

"I don't hate. I don't hate. Give me the Danish."

"Take only one," said the secretary.

But the delivery boy somehow moved the package so quickly that it was on Wanda's desk, and away from the secretary's grabbing hands like a fast ball with a hop.

Ms. Reidel went through the first one in two bites and was into the second before the secretary could get to the white bag spotted with grease and sugar. But Wanda slapped her hand away and was gulping and biting and fending off intrusions. When five Danish were in her stomach and the sixth was big chunks struggling toward her epiglottis, Wanda yelled at her secretary.

"Why did you let me eat these? What the hell is the matter with you?"

The secretary blinked through the hail of semi-chewed Danish that now came at her face along with Ms. Reidel's anger.

"Cunt. Get out of here," yelled Wanda. She futilely threw the white paper bag at her secretary's head. It landed just on the other side of the mother of pearl desk on the turquoise shag rug.

The secretary backed out.

"What are you doing here?"

"I'm here to solve your problem if you solve mine," said the delivery boy.

"A delivery boy solving my problems."

"I'm not just a delivery boy."

"I know. You're going to be a big producer."

"No. All I want is to survive."

"That's what we all want. Why should you survive? What makes you special? Who the hell are you?"

The delivery boy gave a little bow similar to the one he had seen the secretary make when she left the room. Ms. Reidel did not see his hand come down like a pendulum on a pivot. But she did see a corner of her mother of pearl desk crack off evenly, as though sheared.

"You break things, so what? How does that make you any different from furniture movers?"

The delivery boy bowed again, and then, reaching down, picked up the sheared corner of the desk. She saw the orange glow, smelled something like plastic burning, and could have sworn later that those weren't hands on his wrists.

It probably took less than a minute, although at the time it seemed longer. But when the delivery boy backed away from the desktop, she saw a whole, clear, unshattered desk, as flawless as if it had never been cracked.

"How did you do that?"

"The main problem is determining what substance you are dealing with and its comparative fusion rations at variable temperatures, below the combustion level."

"Sure," said Wanda, running her hand over the corner of the desk. It was smooth.

"Sit down, kid," she said. Maybe this delivery boy could help her. After all, wasn't it a busboy who had got her into the men's room at the Brown Derby where she cornered Biff Ballon and wouldn't let him get up or have the toilet paper until he signed. She had stood with her heel on Biff's underwear down by his ankles. Some lesser lights, some jealous ones, might call that crude. But success was never crude.

"Kid," she said, "my problem is this. I've got a beautiful package I'm trying to sell. Perfect. And some studio head is too stupid to see it. What's your solution?"

"While there is some leeway to improve the working of the human mind, basic intelligence does not improve, not even with chemical drugs which affect the species, usually negatively."

"Which means he's not going to change his mind," said Wanda.

"You did not say it was a matter of altering an opinion. That is very possible."

"How?"

"Pain."

"How come you're only a delivery boy, kid?"

"I only appear to be a delivery boy. This I used to enter your office without alarming you."

"Do you love me, kid?"

"Of course not."

"Kid, if you're going to work for me, there's one basic rule you've got to understand. There are times when honesty is definitely not called for."

"Please let me know those times."

"Figure them out for yourself, kid. Now tell me, what kind of pain?"

"Wrenching limbs from sockets creates an enormous pain level in a human. They will do anything to stop that pain."

Wanda Reidel imagined Del Stacey getting his arms torn out of his sockets. She thought of his legs snapping off also. She thought of Del Stacey a writhing trunk on the floor, and she thought of dropping him into a pail of boiling water and seeing if the crustacean really did turn red.

"Did I say something amusing? You are smiling," said Heublein, the delivery boy.

"No, no, just thinking. Uh, do you have something that doesn't kill? You know, sort of just terrorizes."

"Yes, I can create terror."

"Hmmm. And if you get caught, no one would believe a delivery boy's word against mine. Well, no court at least. Let me explain the package I'm trying to sell. An Academy Award director combined with an Academy Award writer along with an actor I know would be super. I just need a little stiffening on the package and then a sell to Stacey."

"What stiffening?"

"The Academy Award director won't talk to me because I don't have Marlon Brando. The Academy Award writer won't talk to anybody. I need them. I already have Biff Ballon."

With an admonition that she wanted to know nothing about how Heublein did it, she gave him the addresses of the writer and the director and told him to take off that silly white jacket.

"If anything goes wrong, I don't know you."

"Oh, you are experienced in self-hypnosis," said Heublein.

"Very," said Wanda Reidel, the Octopussy. "Is Heublein your real name?"

"No."

"What's your real name?"

"Gordons. Mr. Gordons."

"Never heard of anybody changing his name from Gordons. What was it before Gordons?"

"Since I am, it is Gordons."

She gave him a one-page treatment of the movie he should try to sell—to the writer and the director. She already had Biff Ballon.

Walter Mathias Bleekden was catching the Beverly Hills sun while reading *The Wretched of the Earth* when he felt something tug at his left foot, dangling in the lung-shaped swimming pool.

"Stop that, Valerie," he said.

"What did you say?" said his wife, wading through another script she would reject. She sat behind him.

"Oh. I thought you were in the pool. I thought you tugged at my foot."

"No," she said.

"Well, I know that. You're not in the pool."

Suddenly he couldn't move the foot. He yanked, but it wouldn't move. It felt as if it were in a vise.

"Help," yelled Walter Mathias Bleekden and his wife dropped the scripts and ran to the edge of the pool where she saw his foot caught in the chrome ladder. She untangled it and went back to her scripts.

"That chrome ladder wasn't there before," said Bleekden. He was in his late fifties and suntan lotion glistened off the white hair of his chest.

"It must have been, dear," said Valerie.

"I know it wasn't," said Bleekden.

"Maybe it's your white guilt, reading that book."

"I'm through my guilt phase. I'm into my activist phase. Only those who stay beyond the fray should feel guilty. My next picture is going to be significant. Socially and morally significant. I don't have to feel guilt. Guilt is bourgeois."

"Your next picture had better be box office."

"That's what I'm talking about. Morally significant is box office. Black is money. Poverty is money."

"I saw a nice treatment of an Indian theme. There's this wagon train surrounded by the Seventh Cavalry and it's rescued by the Sioux."

But Walter Bleekden did not answer. He was struggling with his beach chair. Somehow his neck was through the webbing and his hands grappled furiously at the arms. Valerie tugged but he could not be freed. Underneath the chair his face turned blue and in the insane moment he could have sworn he heard a voice:

"Phone Wanda Reidel."

It seemed as if it came from the legs of the chair.

"Yes," he gurgled and he felt his wife's hands yanking him free.

"My lord, this is freaky," said Valerie. "What are you doing, strangling yourself?"

"The chair grabbed me."

"Let's get out of the sun, dear," said Valerie.

"It grabbed me."

"Yes, dear. Let's get out of the sun anyhow."

Settled in the spacious living room with leather furniture built into the floor, Walter Mathias Bleekden mixed himself a tall light scotch and, still shaking from the beach chair incident, drank it down. He clapped his hands for his houseboy, who did not appear immediately. If there were two things that bothered Walter Bleekden, it was oppression of racial minorities and uppity servants.

"Where is that houseboy?" grumbled Bleekden.

"He'll be here, dear. After all, this isn't that Wanda Reidel garbage. This is real life."

"What Wanda Reidel? Did you say Wanda Reidel?"

"Yes. She's trying to put together a package with you and that hot young writer, Bertram Mueller. A gross theme. It's a takeoff on Hitchcock's *The Birds*. The furniture and all the surroundings turn against people. Gross. Awful."

"She promised me Marlon Brando. And now she wants to give me Biff Ballon. I won't talk to her."

"You're very wise, dear. It's a loser."

Bleekden nodded. He felt very pleased with himself until later in the day when he went to the bathroom to relieve himself. He opened the door to the bathroom, looked inside and suddenly returned to the living room with his fly still open.

He picked up the silver-handled telephone and dialed.

"Hello, Wanda darling," he said, eyes glazed in terror. "I hear you want to talk to me."

Valerie, surprised, looked in the bathroom. There was the houseboy, kneeling at the bathtub, his shoulders resting on the rim. The bathtub was full. His hair floated above his head at the water line. There were no bubbles coming from his nose or mouth. A massage spray hose was wrapped around his throat.

"Give Wanda my love," yelled Valerie from the bathroom.

Bertram Mueller was finishing a script for Warner Brothers that afternoon when he thought he felt the orange crate move. Mueller typed his work on leftover newsprint using a thirty-five-dollar-and-ninety-eight-cent Woolworth typewriter. His films never failed to gross less than fifteen million dollars, this despite no dialogue ever containing a word with a "Y" in it. That key had broken in the late 1960s when the desk he had built collapsed with the typewriter on it. Normally, such a small fall would not damage even a cheap typewriter, but Mueller had also installed the floor himself.

It took a week to dig the typewriter out of the basement. Mueller hated to waste money on nonessentials. Why spend money on furniture if you could build it yourself? Why waste money on a new typewriter if you could write films that grossed fifteen million each without using a "Y," which wasn't even a legitimate vowel and not much of a consonant either.

Mueller thought it was strange that the crate he sat on moved. He hadn't built the crate.

He looked out over the Pacific from the living room in the newly rented Carmel home for which he paid eight thousand dollars a month. If he was going for eight thousand a month, he certainly wasn't going to squander forty-two dollars on a store-bought chair. Eight thousand a month was more than enough to spend on living quarters, especially when supermarket chains were giving away orange crates.

There was that tug again and now a strangling sensation. He'd have to switch brands of cigarettes. His head felt clouded as if someone were pulling a cord around his neck. The room became dark and he heard the words: "Call Wanda Reidel."

He came to on the floor. That was the first strange incident. Then he discovered that someone had taken his lawnmower and thrown it into the Pacific. The waves lapped up against the handle. And he heard that voice from nowhere again.

"Call Wanda Reidel."

That was a strange thing for a Carmel beach to say.

Back at the house, he phoned Wanda Reidel.

"Are you trying to reach me for something, Wanda?"

"Yes, Bert. I've got the right package for you."

"Not that thing where the environment rebels? What is it called? *Racket Lover*?"

"Bleekden is going to direct it."

"How did you get him?"

"Same way I'm going to get you."

"Are you doing something to my furniture?"

"You know me, Bert. I just try to do my best for my clients. Besides, cardboard boxes aren't anything to worry about."

"My furniture is wood now, if you want to know."

"Stick with me and I'll put you in velvet, love."

"Not with *Racket Lover*."

"Bleekden's in."

"I will not have my name associated with that second-rate farce you're trying to peddle, Wanda," said Mueller.

"Two points off the top," said Wanda, meaning Mueller would get two percent of the film's gross after negative costs.

"It's trash, Wanda."

"Four points, Bert."

"It is an abomination and a waste of time and money and talent. Biff Ballon. Phooey."

"Six points, Bert."

"When do you want the script?" said Bertram Mueller and could have sworn that he heard the phone handle tell him he made the right move, just before Wanda signed off with a "Kiss, kiss."

Before cocktails, Wanda Reidel had put together another "Wandaful package." She made sure she was seen eating out, stopped in on a party to which she was not invited so that those people who viciously asked her how everything was going could be singed to the marrow.

"Just put together a Bleekden-Mueller-Ballon deal with Summit. Today. Glad you asked," said Wanda.

"Great," said the hostess, with a most rewarding gulp, showing her panic at not having invited Wanda in the first place. The anguish of competitors was what made Hollywood worth living in.

"How did you do it, darling?" asked the hostess. "Make a deal with the Mob?"

"Talent, sweetheart," said Wanda, passing up those tempting little bowls of caviar and sour cream, refusing even those crunchies that she normally couldn't resist. She didn't even bother with a midnight snack. She might even become thin.

Of course, there were some worries. Gordons was a find of finds. She'd have to get him signed up, one of those contracts just short of violating the emancipation proclamation. And she'd have to find out what he wanted. Everybody wanted something.

She would handle all that in the morning, she thought. But as she prepared for bed, rubbing her one-hundred-and-seventy-pound, five-foot-four blimp of a frame with Nubody oil that cost thirty-five dollars an ounce—she used a pound a night—she noticed that the door to her bedroom opened quietly behind her. It was Gordons, but now, instead of the white delivery boy's coat, he wore a beige pants suit open to his navel, marcelled hair and a neckchain with half a dozen amulets. She did not ask how he had gotten into her estate or through the electronic guarded door or past the butler. Anyone who could get Bleekden and Mueller through terror in one day could certainly get into her itsy-bitsy eighteen-room mansion.

"Hi, doll," said Gordons.

"You've gone Hollywood, precious," said Wanda.

"I adapt to all situations, love," said Mr. Gordons. "I've done my part in the tradeoff, hon. Now it's your turn."

Wanda turned to uplift her breasts.

"Whatever you want," she said.

And Mr. Gordons explained, telling his life story and his difficulty with the two humans.

"Oh," said Wanda when it was clear he did not want her. She put on a light fuscia gown with ermine collar.

"You have got a problem there, love," said Wanda. "You say this House of Sinanju has lasted a thousand years? More than a thousand?"

"As far as I know," said Mr. Gordons.

"I like what you tried with their boss, Smith. Good thinking."

"It was an attempt. It did not work. Still, it might if they go back and attempt to free him."

"Well, if you're not exactly a normal man, then I

100

shouldn't feel bad that you don't want me physically."

"Correct. It is not a comment on your sexual desirability, love."

"Let's go downstairs to the kitchen," said Wanda. She had ordered that her refrigerators be cleared of all fattening foods and stocked only with garden vegetables and skimmed milk. Therefore Wanda went to the servants' refrigerator and stole their ice cream and doughnuts.

"Creativity, creativity. How do we get you creativity?" She dunked a chocolate-coated doughnut in the fudge ripple. A crust broke off and she ate that with a spoon.

"I have come to a decision about the creativity," said Mr. Gordons. "I have decided that creativity is a uniquely human attribute, and I have resigned myself to doing without it. Instead, I am going to ally myself with a creative person and use that person's creativity to help me attain my goal. You are that person."

"Of course," said Wanda. "But we need a contract. You don't do anything without a contract. You sign with me for say, sixty-five years, with an option for thirty-five more. Not a lifetime contract. That's illegal."

"I will sign any contract you wish. However, precious, you must live up to the bargain," said Mr. Gordons. "The last person who failed to live up to a deal with me is in a refrigerator, love."

"All right, all right. What you need is creative planning. New thought. Original ideas. Boffo dynamite ideas. How do you kill those two guys?"

"Correct," said Mr. Gordons.

"Cement. Put their feet in cement and drop them in a river."

"Won't play in Peoria," said Mr. Gordons who had heard that phrase used recently.

"Blow them up. A bomb in their car."

"Too common," said Mr. Gordons.

"Machine guns?"

"Stale."

"Find a woman to seek out their strength and then betray them?"

"Biblical themes haven't moved since Cecil B. De-Mille," Gordons said.

Wanda went back to the servants' refrigerator. There was a cold pot roast and cream cheese. She spread the cream cheese on a piece of pot roast.

"I have it."

"Yes?"

"Ignore them. They're nobodies. The best revenge is living well."

"I cannot do this. I must destroy them as soon as possible."

"What business are they in again?"

"Assassins, as well as I can determine from the fragmentary information available to me, sweetheart."

"Let's think a little longer," said Wanda. She thought as she ate the pot roast. She thought about what Gordons could do for her. He could help her sign up everybody. All of Hollywood. All of the New York television crowd. She could run the show. And more. He had those computer papers, whatever he called them. They revealed the existence of some secret killer organization. Wanda Reidel could use

102

that to monopolize the press. She would own Page One. Nobody could get in her way.

"Are you done thinking yet?" asked Gordons.

"How old are they again?"

"The white man is in his thirties. The Oriental may be in his eighties. They use traditions passed on from one generation to the next, I believe.

"Traditions, traditions," mused Wanda. She sucked a sinew of pot roast from a lower tooth. "Join their traditions. Adopt them. You said you were adaptable. Become them. Become what they are. Think like them. Act like them."

"I attempted that," said Gordons. "It was why I did not attack the younger one when I had him alone. I thought of what they would do and I decided that if either of them was me, he would wait to get both his targets together. So I waited, and I failed in my attempt to blow them up."

"Have you tried praying?" said Wanda.

"Sweetheart, loved one, precious," said Mr. Gordons, "you're running out of time before I ram that cream cheese through your vestibulocochlear nerve."

"What's that?"

"Your eardrum, love."

"Let's don't be rash. What else do you know about them?"

"The older one is enamored of the daytime television shows."

"Games?"

"No, the story shows."

"Soap operas?"

"They are called that. He particularly likes one

103

called 'As the Planet Revolves,' featuring a person named Rad Rex."

"Rad Rex, *hmmmm?*" said Wanda. "All right. Here's what we do. First, we're going to knock them off one at a time. That's sounder planning."

"If you say so, precious. But how will I be able to do that?"

"You've got to give me a little time to handle that. I've got something in mind. Rad Rex, hmmm?"

8

He had it, and if they wanted it, they were going to pay for it. Dammit, it was that simple to Rad Rex so why wasn't it that simple to his asshole agents at the Maurice Williams Agency too and those goddam assholes at the network.

A half hour show, five days a week, fifty-two weeks a year, and every twittering clit in the country must be watching "As the Planet Revolves" between two thirty and three o'clock every day. Well, if he was going to continue to play Dr. Wyatt Winston—one-time physicist and now a noted surgeon—they were going to pay him for it. That was it. Case closed. *Roma locuta est.*

For heaven's sake, he hoped they didn't think he was playing that insipid macho twit because he liked to. Money. Pure and simple. And if they didn't want to pay for it, let them get somebody else. Try

Rock or Roddy or Rip or Rory. There were plenty of good actors around.

Rad Rex stood up from the violet couch and went to the bar in the leather-walled living room to make himself a banana daiquiri.

He walked carefully, as if he were setting his feet down on two rows of uncooked eggs and trying not to crack them. The overall impression was one of a man who would be at home in ballet slippers.

He hurt, and it was his own fault. He had put on his dark mustache and dark wig to cover his staw-berry-blond curly hair and had gone to a leather bar on the West Side last night and wound up doing a fist number for the rough trade, and he hurt. He would not do that again. This time he meant it. Suppose he had been recognized? Suppose he had wound up with his face smashed?

He put the drink's ingredients in the blender, carefully covered it so nothing would splatter on his green suede suit, then turned the switch. He held his hand on the blender as it whirred the drink to life. He giggled. It felt like a vibrator. He giggled again.

"Vibrators I have known and loved," he said to himself.

"How can one love a vibrator?" The voice was metallic and hollow and sounded to Rad Rex as if a wall were speaking to him. He spun around.

But the apartment was empty. He looked around carefully and felt gooseflesh grow on his shoulders and neck. Empty. But that had been a voice, dammit, a voice.

He swept his eyes around the living room again,

then shrugged. It was getting to him. The pressure of these interminable negotiations over a new contract was just becoming too much.

Rad Rex poured his drink into a Waterford crystal goblet and took it back to the couch, holding the drink away from his side so the condensation didn't drip onto his suit. After the negotiations were over, he was going to take a vacation. That was all. He needed to get away. Two weeks would be nice. Maybe Sausalito. Or Puerto Vallarte. Anyplace where people didn't watch television.

Anyplace where he could be free to be he. Where he could be free to be *he*ing-and-*he*ing.

He giggled again, then stopped, sipped from his daiquiri and spilled a large mouthful all over his green suede trousers when the hollow voice came again: "You have telephone messages."

The voice was very close this time and it *was* metallic. He did not turn around. If the owner of the voice looked like the voice sounded, he did not want to see him.

"Who's there?" he said, staring resolutely at his bar, hoping to catch a glimpse of something in the polished stainless steel door of the refrigerator cabinet, as if a reflection would not be as dangerous to him as an eyes-on view.

"Get your telephone messages," the voice answered.

The telephone was at Rad Rex's right hand. He carefully placed his drink down atop a thin marble coaster on the glass and driftwood table, then pressed the button for the recorder attached to his telephone. As he always did when nervous, he twirled they key he wore on a chain on the left side of his trousers.

The tape whirred, gabbling excitedly backwards, and then the gabbling stopped and he knew he had reached the end of the message. He pressed the talk button and turned up the volume. He stared in the refrigerator door again but saw nothing. He picked up his glass again and sank back into the couch. The velvet cushions were soft, and they enveloped his shoulders like a lover. It was one of the reasons he had designed the couch just that way. To soothe. To relax. For a moment he forgot the voice he thought he had heard.

"Listen to your messages," came the voice again and Rex felt the gooseflesh on his neck and sat up straight. Dammit, this was absurd. He would turn around and see who was talking to him. Imagine, talking to someone in your own living room and being, yes, afraid, to turn around and see who it was. He would turn around. Right now.

He did not turn around.

He sat there and felt the uncomfortable beads of sweat begin to form on his forehead.

The recorder spoke.

"Hiya, Rad, love. Eat anything good lately?"

It was that bitch again, that Wanda Reidel. If he hated anything in the world, it was nasty hard women who acted like men. This was the third call in as many days. Well, he would not call that woman. Agent problem or no agent problem, he simply would not have anything to do with that woman. Not ever.

"This is Wanda, precious one, and I've been trying to reach you for three days." The voice turned sad. "And you haven't called me. I'm beginning to think you don't love me anymore."

The voice paused as if awaiting an answer.

"Well, we'll let bygones be bygones," she said, "because I'm going to do something for you. I know you're having contract problems, Rad honey, and I'm in a position to help you."

Rad Rex sipped his drink. "Sure you are. Probably flat on your back under some network bigshot," he growled softly.

"Just listen," came the metallic voice from somewhere very close to his left ear. He listened.

"I've decided to offer you my services. This will help both of us. First, I'm moving into the New York television market. Second, with my contacts out here on the coast, your next stop is a starring role in films. Celluloid, honey. The real thing. Let's face it. You're too good to spend the rest of your life in a doctor's smock doing five-a-week soaps."

"Go fuck yourself," Rad Rex whispered softly. Not softly enough.

"I will not tell you again, schmuck. Just listen." The metallic voice again.

"Anyway, love, Rad darling, we can help each other. I move into the New York market. You get the best agent in the world and my guarantee, my personal, rock-hard ... that's the way you like it, honey, isn't it—rock hard ... guarantee that your next stop is a film. A budget biggie. No crap. What can those shlubs at Maurice Williams do for you like that? What have they done for you? Remember, sweets, they've got a lot of their people on contract

109

with your network. You think they're going to rock the boat? Fight for you and hurt their other clients?"

The Octopussy had struck a nerve. It was probably true, Rad Rex thought. Probably true. Those bastards at the agency were selling him out, just to protect some nickel and dimers. Trade off old Rad Rex. Get him to work for spit and the network brass would wink and promise, without ever having to say a word, that they'd make it up to the agency with some of the other contracts coming up for renegotiation. Oh, those dirty bastards. It was true. Rad Rex knew it was true. If only Wanda Reidel weren't such a pushy bitch.

"Anyway, love, I'm sending my right-hand man, a Mr. Gordons, to come and see you. He'll have a contract with him. Sign it like a good boy, and then Wanda will have her crack at that network brass. But remember the big picture, Rad. The big picture. For you, it's Hollywood. Significance. Fame. Power. They're waiting for you, honey." She paused. "Kiss, kiss. And if it's really good looking, kiss it for me, too."

She laughed a braying laugh, and then the recorder clicked itself off.

"Cesspool cunt," said Rad Rex, finishing his drink.

"That is no way to speak about your benefactress."

Rad Rex still did not turn around. "Are you this Mr. Gordon?" he asked, carefully placing his empty goblet on the marble coaster.

"The name is Mr. Gordons. Yes, I am he."

Rad Rex turned around casually on the sofa, moving slowly, allowing himself to be able to recoil swiftly if he should have to.

The look of nervous apprehension on his face changed smoothly to a smile when he saw the man standing there. He was in his mid-thirties with light blond hair, carefully curled over his forehead in a Caesar cut. The man wore a tan suede jacket and dark brown linen slacks and open-toed sandals without socks. He was shirtless and his jacket was open, and on his bare chest he wore a huge silver pendant with an equal sign inscribed on it.

But what brought the smile was the man's key. He wore a plain gold key, hanging from a small chain that draped into his left front pocket and while many people wore many kinds of things nowadays which not did not really tell you a great deal about them, the key in the left pocket meant something very specific to Rad Rex. Mr. Gordons was a kindred spirit.

Rad Rex stood up and smiled, trying to dazzle Mr. Gordons with his display of orthodontia. Yes, Mr. Gordons was a good-looking young man. And he looked soft. It might be nice.

"Can I offer you a drink?"

"I do not drink," said Mr. Gordons. He did not smile back. "I have brought a contract from Wanda."

He held up a sheaf of papers in his right hand. Rex put up a hand in dismissal. "Plenty of time to talk about that later, love. You don't mind if I have one, do you?"

"Your drinking habits are no concern of mine."

God, it was eerie how the voice was clipped and precise and almost sounded as if it came from a robot. "I have come to have you sign this contract."

Rad Rex smiled to himself. He was not going to be pushed into signing any contract. The last time he had been pushed into anything was a few years earlier when a gang of Mafia goons had shown up at his studio and caused labor trouble and raised hell and finally forced Rad Rex to write a message on a picture of himself that was going to a fan. At the time it had been frightening. Later it became silly. The Mafia? For an autographed picture? Ridiculous. But at the time, Rex was scared.

He was younger then. He would not be pushed anymore. Not by the network, not by Wanda Reidel, not by this Mr. Gordons, no matter how cute he was.

Rex pushed the ingredients into his blender and made another daiquiri. He turned again to face Mr. Gordons, leaning back against the bar on his left elbow, legs crossed at the ankles, holding his glass in his right hand, away from the suit, eyelids set at sleepy half-mast, faint smile on his lips.

"I hope drinking is the only vice you don't have," he said softly.

"All right, fag," said Mr. Gordons. "My tolerance with you is about to end. You may finish consuming your drink and then you will sign this contract."

"Hold on, fella," said Rex. Not fag. He wasn't going to be called that. Not in his own apartment. "You don't have to be here you know. I'll throw you out on your sweet little heinie." He pointed to the wall behind Mr. Gordons from which hung a karate gi and an assortment of yawara sticks, Oriental hand-fighting implements. "Those are mine, pal. I'm a black belt so just watch it, or you'll be out on your duff."

"I will be no such thing. You will sign this contract."

"Fuck off," said Rad Rex. Forget him. Mr. Gordons' key was a fake. He was a fake, working for a fake, and Rex was not going to bother with fakes. He carefully unarranged his legs, turned from Mr. Gordons and sat on a stool at the bar. He set his glass down on the wooden bar top. He looked at his face in the refrigerator door. He saw Mr. Gordons move slowly and silently alongside him.

Let him. Rad Rex would not turn around. He would not dignify this imposter twerp by arguing with him. Let him go back to Hollywood and sink a pork injection into that disgusting Octopussy that he worked for. Let him argue. Let him plead. Rad Rex was immovable, as unchanging as the very gods.

Mr. Gordons did not try to argue with Rad Rex. He reached his hand in front of the actor and encircled the Waterford goblet. Rex watched the delicate, almost hairless hand settle around the glass. Good. Maybe he was going to loosen up. He turned to look at Mr. Gordons, a small flicker of good-natured hope at the corners of his mouth. Mr. Gordons was not smiling and not looking at him. He was looking at his own right hand on the goblet.

Crack! The sound startled Rex. He looked back at Mr. Gordons' hand. The glass had been crushed. The yellow goop of the daiquiri puddled on the bar top.

Chunks of expensive crystal sat in the spilled drink, like miniature icebergs in a thick yellow sea.

Mr. Gordons still had much of the glass in his hand. Rex watched, fascinated, as Gordons continued to squeeze. He could hear the big glass chips cracking into smaller glass chips. God. That was it. The man was a pain freak. A blood nut. His hand must be like hamburger now. The breaking crystal sounded like the tinkle of very small bells very far away.

Mr. Gordons opened his hand slowly. The expensive Irish crystal was now reduced to a dull white powder, uniform and small, almost like table salt. Gordons dropped the powder onto the bar. Rex looked in astonishment. Mr. Gordons' hand was unmarked. Not a cut. Not a scratch. Not a drop of blood.

He looked at Gordons. Gordons looked at him.

"I can do the same thing to your skull, fag. Now sign the contract."

Rex looked at the pile of crystal dust on the bar. He looked at the unmarked palm of Mr. Gordons' right hand and he reached over the bar for a pen and began to sign the three copies of the contract without even reading them.

Wetness collected along his lower back near the base of his spine. He could not remember the last time he had felt that unpleasant moisture.

Yes, he could. It was that day years before with those Mafia goons who wanted that picture autographed. What was it he had written that day? An autographed picture to a special fan.

He remembered the inscription because he had done it twice before he had gotten it right.

114

"Chiun. To the wisest, most wonderful, kindheart-
ed, humble, sensitive gift of man. Undying respect.
Rad Rex."

Strange he should think of that now.

9

Gerald O'Laughlin Flinn signaled the waiter for another round of Bloody Marys.

"Not me, dearest," said Wanda Reidel. "One's my limit when I'm working."

Flinn flashed her a smile so bright it looked as if his teeth had been painted with refrigerator enamel. "Oh," he said casually, "you're working today? And I thought this was just a social call."

Wanda Reidel smiled back, a smile as warm as a codfish's skin.

"And you're as full of shit as a Christmas goose," she said, still smiling and using the tine of her appetizer fork to pluck a piece of Alaskan king crab from between two right front teeth. "When an agent like me and the number one negotiations honcho for a big network like you get together, it's always business."

The waiter with the name tag "Ernesto" returned with the two drinks. Flinn took them from the tray and put them both in front of his own plate.

"Would you like anything, dear?" he asked Wanda.

She looked up at the waiter, a young, well-groomed vaguely foreign man with dark wavy hair and skin with a faint olive tinge.

"There are a lot of things I'd like," she said, her eyes fixed on the young waiter's, "but they'll have to wait." The waiter smiled and nodded. He turned away.

"Just a minute," she said. He turned back.

"I'll have a dish of ice cream. What kind of ice cream do you have?"

"What kind would Mademoiselle desire?" the young man asked in flavored English.

"Mademoiselle, God, Mademoiselle would like rum raisin." She turned to Flinn. "Do you know I haven't had rum raisin ice cream in twenty years? Do you know I'd do anything for a dish of rum raisin?" Back to the waiter. "Anything. I don't suppose you have rum raisin."

"We will locate some for Mademoiselle," the young waiter said and moved smoothly away into the kitchen where he said to the maitre'd in a voice that was all Bronx: "You sure that bitch is worth all this trouble?"

"That bitch can buy and sell you and seven generations of your family, Ernie," said the maitre'd.

"Then I gotta go over to Baskin-Robbins and find some rum raisin ice cream. She wants rum raisin ice cream, for Christ's sake. Nobody eats rum raisin ice cream. What's wrong with that tub of shit?"

117

"If she wants rum raisin, you find rum raisin," said the maitre'd.

As Ernie went to the door, the maitre'd called, "If Baskin-Robbins doesn't have it, find the nearest Howard Johnsons. Hurry up. Take a cab if you have to. And while you're looking, I'll mix some up."

"Mix it up?"

"I guess so," the maitre'd shrugged. "What's in it? Vanilla, rum, and raisins, I guess. We'll try. But you try to get it first."

"How much do you want?" asked the waiter.

"Better get a gallon. She ate three portions of king crab. That garbage pail'll probably eat the whole gallon."

Back at the table, Gerald O'Laughlin Flinn finished half of the first Bloody Mary and said, "Well, if this is business, what is this business about?"

"Rad Rex."

"Oh, yes," said Flinn, reminding himself to be cautious. "Very pleasant, fellow, Rad. But he seems to have some inflated ideas of the economics of daytime television." He looked at Wanda, blandly wondering what the Octopussy wanted with him and why she was interested in Rad Rex. Christ, the fruitcake wasn't even a stud for her.

Wanda smiled. "I suppose he gets those ideas from reading his thousands of fan letters each week."

Flinn shrugged. "You know the type who writes fan letters to soap opera stars. Demographically, zeroes. Not worth spit. They don't have enough money to buy anything, and even if they did, they couldn't find their way to the grocery store."

"Demographics is a lot of shit," said Wanda.

"Anyway," said Flinn, finishing off the rest of the first Bloody Mary neatly. "We're very close to a contract with Maurice Williams for Rad's services. How does it all interest you?"

"First. You're a liar. You and Maurice Williams are a million miles apart on a contract. Second. More important. Maurice Williams is out." She looked up from the plate, a tiny driblet of crabmeat sticking from the side of her mouth like the tail of a small fish being swallowed by a barracuda. "They're out. I'm in. I'm Rad's new agent."

The polish peeled off Gerald O'Laughlin Flinn as if he had just been dipped in lemon juice.

"Oh, shit," he said.

Wanda smiled. "Now, now, love. It might not be as bad as all that."

Flinn picked up the extra Bloody Mary. If he had drunk it, it would have been his third for lunch. But instead he fingered the glass, then placed it back down on the table, inches away from where it had been, but farther from him, symbolically out of reach. One did not swill down Bloody Marys when getting ready to negotiate with the Octopussy, or more blood might wind up being spilled.

He shrugged. "I didn't mean that against you," he said. "It's just that it's difficult to be negotiating for months with one agency and then have to start all over again with another. Do you know the minor points we've worked out? Hundreds probably. That's hundreds of points you and I'll have to start all over again on."

Wanda searched for another scrap of crabmeat. Finding none, she used the side of her fork to scoop

119

some of the thick red horseradished cocktail sauce into her mouth. An errant spot of sauce dropped on her chin and remained there for a few seconds until Wanda could put down the fork and pick up the napkin. Flinn looked at the red droplet and said to himself, This women's going to kill me. This women's going to eat me alive.

Wanda answered the unspoken thought. "It just won't be that bad, Gerry. Not that bad."

"That's what you say."

She put her napkin down briskly. She pushed her plate away from her toward the center of the table. It clinked heavily against the base of the full Bloody Mary glass. She folded her hands on the table in front of her, like a seven-year-old sitting in church, waiting to make first Holy Communion.

"First," she said, "the hundreds of points you negotiated already. The hundreds. Thousands. I don't give a shit. They stand. All right by me."

Flinn's eyes widened slightly.

"Right," she said. "I don't care. They stand. Now. What's Rad making now in the series?"

"Sixteen hundred dollars a week," said Flinn.

"What's Maurice Williams been asking?" said Wanda.

"Three thousand a week."

"What have you offered?" asked Wanda. She kept her eyes riveted on Flinn's so he could not look away, could not turn his head to find a lie or half-truth floating around somewhere near the ceiling and snatch it up for use.

No point in lying, Flinn thought. She could check it out anyway.

"We've offered twenty-two hundred a week."

"We'll take it," said Wanda.

She smiled at Flinn's open look of shock. "Now that wasn't so difficult, was it?" She looked around. "Where is that cute little swordsman with my ice cream?"

Flinn did not care about her ice cream. Right then he did not care about anything except the prospect of rapidly getting Rad Rex's name on a contract. His right hand reached out and fondled the Bloody Mary. "Just like that? You'll take twenty-two hundred a week?"

"Just like that. We'll take twenty-two hundred a week."

Almost of its own volition, Flinn's right hand brought the full Bloody Mary up close to his mouth and he took a long swallow. He could not remember ever enjoying a taste more. So this was the great Wanda Reidel? The Octopussy? More like a kitty cat, he thought. She was easy. He smiled. She smiled back.

"But there are a couple of little things I need. Just to sweeten the pot. To show Rad I'm really working for him."

Flinn put the drink back down. "What kind of little things?"

"Rad's got to have some schedule flexibility, so that when I get him a picture, he'll be able to make it."

"What about the shows during that period?"

"I'm not asking for time off for him. He'll double up and tape extra shows before the movie filming starts. I don't want time off. I said flexibility. I mean flexibility."

121

"You got it," said Flinn. "Any other little things?"

Wanda shook her head. "Not that I can think of right now."

Ernie returned with the rum raisin ice cream he had bought in Baskin-Robbins.

"For Mademoiselle," he said, placing the china bowl in front of her.

She lifted it and sniffed. "Wonderful, love," she said. "Now I want whipped cream. Real whipped cream. None of that spray crap. And nuts. Walnuts. And chocolate syrup."

"As Mademoiselle wishes." The waiter walked away.

Behind him, Wanda Reidel met Gerald O'Laughlin Flinn's eyes again. She spooned a massive lump of ice cream, the size of a Great Dane dropping, into her mouth. With little streamlets of the ice cream slipping out of the corners of her mouth and dribbling down toward her chin like two tan fangs, she said slowly: "There is just one more little thing, come to think of it."

"You've sold me out. You've sold me out. You've sold me out." Rad Rex's litany started in his usual on-camera baritone and ended in an anguished soprano squeak.

He spun in the pink chair away from the mirror in his dressing room at the television studio on West Fifty-sixth Street in Manhattan, came around to face Wanda Reidel, and for emphasis, stamped his foot.

"You've sold me out," he complained again. "That's it. You're fired."

"Sorry, love, you can't fire me," said Wanda. "No-cut contract. Exclusive. Three years. Without me, you don't work."

"I won't sign with the network. Not for twenty-two hundred a week."

"You don't have to sign," said Wanda. "I already did. Your contract with me empowers me to approve and sign contracts."

"I won't work. I won't, I tell you." Rex's face brightened. "I'll get laryngitis. I'll get the longest case of laryngitis in history. Protracted. It'll go on for months."

"Try fucking around with fake laryngitis and I'll have Mr. Gordons take out your voice box to see if it can't be repaired," said Wanda sweetly. "Don't worry, You'd still be able to work. The silents might come back. Maybe you could even do the life of Marcel Marceau."

"You can't do this to me. This is America." Rad Rex's eyes glistened. His voice seemed to falter.

"No, love. To you, it's America. To me, it's the jungle. Now stop sniveling and look at the good side."

"There isn't any good side."

"I got you time to make a movie, and I'm lining up a great deal for you."

"Big deal. I've got to do double shows."

"So what? It'll be easy for you. You're a quick study."

"And what is this other poop?" asked Rex. "This three-minute spot?"

"That's something very important," said Wanda. "Today, your show's going to be cut by three minutes. After the commercials, you get three minutes to read a message to the audience."

"What message? What do I want to say to a lot of housewives?"

Wanda dug into a straw handbag that looked as if it had been recycled from a Mexican family's sandals.

"You just read this."

She handed Rad Rex a sheet of paper. He looked at it quickly. "What is this crap?"

"The crap you're going to read."

"In a pig's poopoo, I am. It doesn't make any sense."

"Just do it. Consider it a favor."

"For you? Hah!"

"For Mr. Gordons."

Rad Rex looked at Wanda's bland eyes again, then down at the paper, scanning it rapidly, committing the phrases to memory.

Remo sat sprawled in the armchair in their motel room in Burwell, Nebraska.

His legs were stretched out in front of him, and he was keeping time with his big toes to the beat of an invisible drummer. He was bored. To the depth and breadth of his soul, he was bored. Bored, bored, bored.

Already that morning, he had done his finger stands; he had practiced the floater stroke and had not dislocated a shoulder, although he would have almost been glad to, if only to relieve the monotony. He had done his breathing exercises, pulling his respiration down to two breaths a minute. He had worked on his pulse, lowering it to twenty-four and raising it to ninety-six. In his mind, he had done his roadwork, running through a virgin forest in the great Northwest, slipping up quietly on animals, racing with them, usually winning. He had come out of it after he had run into a great doe, a giant female deer, and had begun to think the beast was attractive. That was when he realized how bored he was.

Even his toes were bored.

Seven days in this town would bore anyone. Strange, it never seemed to bore the people who lived in these kind of towns. Maybe it was because they knew more about their towns than he did. One of the perils of being an outsider. Remo Williams, perpetual outsider. Outside everybody. Outside everyplace. No family, no home, no goals.

Strike that. He did have family. It sat in front of him now on the floor, wearing a ceremonial blue afternoon robe, eyes riveted to the television set where Dr. Whitlow Wyatt was revealing to Mr. Brace Riggs that her husband Elmore's disease was fatal. However, Dr. Wyatt had heard of a serum. A very rare serum, prepared in the depths of the equatorial jungle by natives from an herb which they grew secretly. But the serum was unavailable to Western medicine. "We cannot get any?" asked Mrs. Riggs, who loved her husband, even if she had for fourteen years, been having an affair with the Episcopalian priest in town, Father Daniel Bennington. But Dr. Wyatt assured her that there was a chance—a slim chance. If Dr. Wyatt himself went and confronted the headhunting Jivaro Indians, perhaps with an appeal to a greater morality he could coax from them some of the serum.

"You would go?" said Mrs. Riggs.

"I would go," said Dr. Wyatt.

"Go," said Remo. "And keep going."

The organ music came up and over, and the program faded.

Chiun wheeled on Remo. "See what you did?"

"What did I do?"

"They made this show too short. It is three minutes too short."

"I didn't have anything to . . ."

"Shhh," said Chiun as an announcer came on screen.

"In just a moment, Rad Rex—the star of 'As the Planet Revolves'—will have a special word for special members of our viewing audience. But first these messages."

"You are lucky, Remo," said Chiun.

"Well, as long as I'm lucky, try this. We're leaving. We're going back to get Smith out of that room. No more just sitting here going out of our minds."

"And Mr. Gordons?"

"Screw Mr. Gordons. I'm not going to spend my life hiding while you put into motion some hundred-year program for dealing with him. We'll go find him."

"How like a child," said Chiun. "To choose an obvious guaranteed catastrophe because he is too bored to wait for a better moment." He tried to mimic Remo's American accent, lowering his voice so he sounded like a flute trying to play bass. "Don't matter what happens, pard. Just as long as it happens fast."

"Are you done with the impersonations, Little Father?" said Remo.

"Yeah, Stumpy," said Chiun again in the deep voice, imitating a line from a John Wayne movie.

Since Remo was bigger than Chiun by a foot and heavier by more than fifty pounds, this made him laugh despite his annoyance.

"Stop that cackling," ordered Chiun suddenly. He turned his attention back to the television where Rad Rex's face appeared in closeup. He still wore his doctor's robes. His face, Remo thought, looked glum, not like the healthy smile he wore on that autographed photo of him that Chiun had terrorized the Mafia into providing a few years earlier.

Rex began to talk slowly.

"Friends, it is a pleasure to let you know that I will continue in the role of Dr. Whitlow Wyatt on 'As the Planet Revolves.'" He paused.

"Hooray," Chiun cheered.

"Silence," said Remo.

"Coming into the homes of so many of you every day has been the biggest thrill of my life," Rex said, "and I look forward to continuing with you, trying to bring you good stories about real people caught in the real problems of real life.

"Some people like to sneer at our daytime dramas, to call them foolish and insignificant. But I know better. I know the lives these stories have touched and brightened.

"And even if my own faith were in doubt, I would be reassured by the knowledge that out there, in television land, there is one who knows. Out there, there is a man of such wisdom and strength and humility and beauty and he approves of what we do here. It is to that person that these shows are directed, because it is from the knowledge of his support that I gain the strength to go on.

"I am now going to Hollywood for a brief period. Some of you may have heard that I may soon make a film, but I want you all to know that 'As the Planet Revolves' will continue.

"So now I am off to Hollywood. And I hope that there I will have the opportunity to meet in person the man I have heard so much about, the man who understands what it is I do, and that I will have the chance to sit at his feet and soak in his wisdom."

Rad Rex looked up and with a small smile directly into the camera, he said: "Beloved Master, I wait for you in Hollywood."

His face faded, and there were a few seconds of pause before the commercials came on again.

"That's it," said Chiun.

"That's what?" asked Remo.

"We are not staying in this room anymore. We are going to Hollywood."

"Why would we go to Hollywood?" asked Remo, "Assuming for a moment, inaccurately, that we were actually going to Hollywood."

"Because Rad Rex is waiting there for me."

"You think that message was directed to you?"

"You heard it. He said wisdom, strength, humility and beauty. Who else do you know that he could have been talking about?"

"He was probably talking about his hairdresser."

"He was speaking to me," said Chiun, rising to his feet so smoothly that the robe seemed almost not to stir. "I will leave you to make the arrangements for our trip to Hollywood. I will hold you personally

128

responsible if we should fail to meet Rad Rex for any reason. I must go and pack."

Chiun swept from the room, a half-second before the trail of his robe caught up with him. Remo saw the bedroom door close behind Chiun and sank even deeper into his chair.

"Chiun," he yelled.

"That is my name," piped back the voice from the other room.

"Why should Rad Rex send a message to you?"

"Perhaps he has heard of me. Many know of the Masters of Sinanju. Not all are as stupid as you once were."

Remo sighed. "Why do you think he wants to meet you?" he yelled.

"To see for himself what perfection is."

Remo nodded in disgust. Just what Chiun needed. More stroking. It was like that dippy mail he kept getting at that Massachusetts post office box, and which he made Remo read to him. "Oh, wonderful, glorious, magnificent, et cetera, et cetera," Remo would read, and Chiun would sit on the floor, nodding agreement. After a month of that, Remo had taken to changing the letters slightly.

"Dear Chiun. You are an arrogant, self-centered obnoxious person who does not recognize the true worth of your adopted son, Remo."

Chiun had looked up. "Discard that one. The writer is obviously deranged and they may not allow him to receive letters in the place where he is stabled."

After a few more, however, Chiun began to observe that Remo was not reading the letters with

129

any great amount of accuracy and had taken over again the task of reading them himself.

And now, more stroking, this time on expensive television. From Rad Rex, yet.

Why? Remo asked himself.

And Remo answered himself: because of Mr. Gordons. It is his way to get us to Hollywood, where he can attack.

And aloud he called to Chiun, "Chiun, we're going to Hollywood."

Chiun reappeared in the bedroom doorway.

"Of course we are. Did you ever doubt it?"

"You know why?" asked Remo.

"Because I want to. That would be reason enough for someone who understands gratitude. What is your reason?"

"Because we're going to find Mr. Gordons there."

"Really?" said Chiun.

"Because Rad Rex is working in cahoots with that box of bolts."

"You really think so, Remo?" said Chiun.

"I know so."

"Oh, how wise you are. How fortunate I am to be with you."

He turned away and reentered the bedroom. From inside, Remo could hear him say faintly: "Idiot."

10

"Look, look! There is Clark Clable."

"His name is not Clark Clable, Chiun. It's Clark Gable. With a *G*."

"Look, look! There is Clark Gable."

"It's not Clark Gable," Remo said. "Clark Gable is dead."

"You just told me it was Clark Gable."

"I told you his *name* was Clark Gable," said Remo as he felt the sands of reasoned discourse slowly sift away from under his feet.

"If his name is Clark Gable, isn't that the same as being Clark Gable?" Chiun asked.

"Please eat your rice," said Remo.

"I will. I will. I will do anything rather than speak to a person who lies to me." He raised a spoonful of rice to his mouth, then dropped the spoon on his plate.

"Look, look! There is Barbra Streisand." Chiun's voice was more excited than Remo had ever heard it before. His right index finger trembled as it pointed across the room. Remo followed the direction of the finger.

"Chiun, that's a waitress, for Christ's sake."

"As you often say, so what? Maybe Barbara Streisand has a new job."

"Waitressing in her spare time?"

"Why not?" asked Chiun. "Remember you this, white man. There is no glory in any job; there is glory only in the person who works in that job, no matter how slight it might seem. Not all can be assassins." He looked again at the girl in the black waitress uniform who stood across the room, totalling up a check. "That is Barbra Streisand," he said with finality.

"Go ask her to sing for you," said Remo disgustedly. He felt rather than heard or saw Chiun move away and when he turned back, the old man was walking slowly toward the waitress. It had been like this for two days. Chiun, noble and venerable master of the ancient and illustrious House of Sinanju, was star-struck. It started in the airport when he thought he saw Johnny Mack Brown pushing a broom. In the cab, he thought the driver was Ramon Navarro. He was convinced that the desk clerk at the Sportsmen's Lodge where they were staying was Tony Randall, and finally, he had accused Remo of maliciously attempting to deprive an old man of a few moments of joy by denying who all these people were.

Since Barbara Streisand was the great unrequited love of Chiun's life, Remo did not want to watch the waitress's putdown. It would be too painful. He turned and looked out the window at the small trout stream which meandered between the restaurant and the main building of the lodge, less than a hundred feet from a major highway in a concrete-smothered section of Hollywood.

Remo wondered when Mr. Gordons would come after them. It was bad enough dealing with a man who could have an edge through surprise. But Mr. Gordons wasn't a man; he was a self re-creating android who was an assimilator. He could assume any shape. He could be the beds in their room; he could be the chair Remo sat in. These things were not beyond Gordons' abilities.

And worse, Chiun didn't seem to care, resolutely refusing to admit that Rad Rex was in any way connected with Mr. Gordons.

Remo's inspection of the trout stream was interrupted when a high sound like a strong breeze flicking through tall nighttime trees sailed through the restaurant. It was a woman's voice, singing. He turned back to look at Chiun. The singing had ended as abruptly as it had started. Chiun stood by the waitress, for it had been she singing. Chiun smiled and nodded. She nodded back. Chiun raised his hands toward her as if in a blessing, then returned to Remo, his face wreathed in a beatific smile.

Remo looked past him at the waitress. A waitress?

Chiun sat gently in his chair and without a word lifted his spoon and plunged it into his rice. His appetite had returned, amazingly strong.

Remo stared at him. Chiun, chewing, smiled.

"Nice voice she has," said Remo.

"You really think so?" asked Chiun blandly.

"Sounds like . . . you know who," said Remo.

"No. I do not know who," said Chiun.

"You know. Like . . . her."

"It could not be her. After all, she is but a waitress. You told me so yourself."

"Yeah, but maybe she's making a film here or something."

"Perhaps. Why not go ask her?" suggested Chiun.

"Aaah, she'd probably laugh at me," Remo said.

"Why not? Doesn't everyone?"

"Swallow spit," said Remo.

11

Remo called Smith from their hotel room, and the bed-bound director of CURE demanded to know where Remo was.

"Hollywood. I'm having fun in Hollywood," sang Remo in an offkey baritone.

"Hollywood?"

"Hollywood," said Remo.

"That's wonderful," said Smith, dripping sarcasm. "And here I thought you might be wasting your time. And what of me? I would like to get out of this room."

"Just a minute," said Remo. He looked to where Chiun was standing in front of the sheer curtains, looking out the window toward the swimming pool.

Remo did not bother to cover the mouthpiece.

"Chiun," he said. "Smitty wants to get out of the hospital room."

"Smith may do what he wants," said Chiun, without turning. "The master of Sinanju is otherwise occupied."

Remo's eyes narrowed maliciously. He extended the open telephone toward Chiun and said sweetly, "You mean you don't care what happens to Smith?"

He extended the phone as far as he could as Chiun answered, still without turning.

"The activities of even an emperor pale into insignificance when compared with my searching for my own destiny."

"And your destiny involves Rad Rex?" Remo said.

"Precisely," said Chiun.

"In other words," Remo said, "Rad Rex, the television actor, is more important to you than Dr. Smith and the organization?"

"On most days," Chiun said, "the weather forecast is more important to me than Dr. Smith and the organization." He turned. He saw the open telephone in Remo's hand and the nasty tight-lipped smile on Remo's face. He glared at Remo.

"But those feelings last only a moment," Chiun said loudly. "They are a sign of my personal weakness because in moments I again realize how important the great Emperor Smith and his wonderful organization are to the world and I praise the fates that have brought me into his employ even in so lowly a position as trainer to a pale piece of pig's ear. All hail Emperor Smith. The Master is attempting to think of a way to release him from that explosive trap. The answer will surely be here in California. All hail the noble Smith."

Remo scowled at Chiun's fancy footwork and

talked into the telephone again. "Another precinct heard from. Another loyal servant of the great emperor."

"Remo, I can't stay here forever. I'm tired of using bedpans and not leaving my room for fear it'll explode as I go through the door. Who knows what the hell is going on back at the office without me?"

Remo felt sympathy for Smith. The man had almost been blown to death; he was living now inside a bomb that could be triggered by God knew what, and his complaint was that he had to get back to the office to get his work done.

"Smitty, look. Stick it out a couple more days. Gordons is here. If we don't nail him right away, we'll be back to get you out."

"All right. But hurry, will you?"

"Sure, sweetheart," said Remo. "That's Hollywood talk."

Remo's second call was to a television network public relations agency in New York, where he found that Rad Rex was under exclusive agency contract to Wanda Reidel.

His third call was to Wanda Reidel's office.

"Ms. Reidel's office."

"I'm looking for Rad Rex," Remo said.

"And who might you be?" The secretary's voice was chilly.

"I might be Sam Goldwyn," said Remo. He began to continue "but I'm not," but before he could, the secretary was gushing apologies to Mr. Goldwyn and she was sorry and don't worry, Mr. Goldwyn, Ms. Reidel would be on the phone right away, and then there was a pause and a woman's brash voice jumped onto the phone and said, "Sam, baby, honey, I didn't think they had phone service in the grave."

"Actually," said Remo, "I'm not . . ."

"I know who you're not, love. The question is who you are."

"I've got business with Rad Rex."

"Your name?" said Wanda.

"I use a lot of names, but you can just call me the Master." This lie was rewarded by Chiun glaring at Remo from across the room.

"You don't sound like the Master," said Wanda.

"And how does the Master sound?"

"High-pitched, squeaky voice. Oriental, almost a British accent. Peter Lorre doing Mr. Moto."

"Well, actually, I'm the Master's assistant." Remo bit his lip. Chiun nodded in agreement.

"Give me a name, love."

"How's Remo?"

"It'll do. I'll see you whenever you get here," said Wanda. "Kiss, kiss."

The phone clicked in Remo's ear.

"Shit, shit," said Remo.

There was only one major obstacle to Remo's meeting privately with Wanda Reidel. Chiun.

The Master wanted to see the woman who would bring him and Rad Rex together. Remo, on the other hand, wanted to talk what he hoped would be sense with Wanda Reidel, and therefore it was imperative that Chiun be included out.

The irresistible force of Chiun's wishes and the immovable object of Remo's stubbornness was solved by Remo putting Chiun aboard a bus, with a promise from the busdriver that he would take Chiun on a tour of the homes of all the famous

138

people in Hollywood. Meanwhile, Remo would do a good clerk's work and find out where Chiun was to meet Rad Rex.

As he was putting Chiun on the bus, Remo thought of so many times from his childhood, being put on the orphanage bus by nuns to go visit places, places owned and inhabited by people with names, with families, with pasts and presents and futures, and he remembered what he looked like then and asked Chiun suddenly, "Do you want me to make you a nice little sandwich in a brown paper bag?"

But Chiun only hissed at him that he should not forget himself and then clambered aboard the giant blue-and-white bus that was already filled with other Hollywood sightseers who were paying three fifty each for the privilege of riding through the streets of Beverly Hill and being gawked at by the townies, who thought they looked funny, and by the pimps, who were ever alert for fresh young meat who might easily be convinced that the way to a movie contract was through a producer's bed and, yes, that the man with the big belly and the twenty-dollar bill was really one of the biggest producers in the world, even if he did say he was a tie salesman from Grand Rapids, Michigan . . .

In turn the people on the bus gawked back at the townies, who they thought also looked funny and at the pimps because they just knew by the pimps' clothes and cars that they had to be big stars, never realizing that in a town built on stardom, that lived for stardom, the real stars were the only ones who didn't dress like stars. In another town, wearing jeans or slacks and sneakers and doing your own shopping would be a perfect way for a star to melt into the background, to become invisible. But in California, Hollywood-style, it worked in reverse, and the real star-watchers kept their eyes peeled for people who looked dull. And ordinary. And so the cloak of disguise turned out to be a neon light blinking overhead that raucoused, look at me, look at me, here I am.

Which was, after all, just what the stars wanted, their parallel to the Howard Hughes' I-don't-want-any-publicity gambit which had guaranteed him the most intensive press coverage of any almost-living man in the world.

Wanda Reidel was a different matter. She dressed like a slob, not by design, not to call attention to herself, but because she didn't have the sense to know she wasn't beautifully decked out. She thought she looked great; Remo thought she looked like the wife of the owner of an East Fourth Street lighting fixtures store.

Her wrists jangled and clattered with bracelets as she pointed a purple fingernail at Remo, who sat in a suede chair across from her desk, and demanded: "What do you want, love? I thought you were on the level, but with those bones in your face, don't tell me you're not an actor."

Remo resisted the urge to shout, "Just a break, Ms. Reidel. Just a break. I'll do anything for a break," and instead said only, "I'm looking for Mr. Gordons."

"Mister who?"

"Listen, love, precious, sweetheart, honey, dear, and darling. Let's cut through all the bullshit. You represent Rad Rex. You had him tape that crap to

get my partner and me out here. The only person
... scratch that, thing that wants my partner and
me out here is Mr. Gordons. You didn't make a cent
from Rex's message, so you did it because Gordons
told you to. It's that simple. That gets us up to now.
Where's Gordons?"

"You know you've got something."

"Yeah. A nervous stomach."

"You've got rich intensity. You've got the looks.
The ability to sound hard. Manly, but without
macho. Come on. A screen test. What do you say?
Don't tell me you never thought about one?"

"I have, I have," admitted Remo. "But then when
they gave Sidney Greenstreet that part in *The
Maltese Falcon* it took the heart right out of me, and
I gave up and went back to what I do best."

"Which is?"

"Which is none of your business. Where's
Gordons?"

"Suppose I told you he was that chair you're
sitting on?"

"I'd tell you you were full of crap."

"You sure you know Mr. Gordons?"

"I know him. I can smell the diesel fuel when he's
around. I can hear the tiny click-clicking of electri-
cal connections in that make-believe brain. He
smells like a new car. There's none of that here. Tell
me, what are you doing with him anyway?"

And as soon as Remo asked the question, he had
the feeling, the frightening feeling, that this dippo
facing him might just be trying to promote Mr.
Gordons into a movie contract. The incredible changing man. Mr. Chameleon. Supertool.

"You're not planning a movie, are you?" he asked warily.

Wanda Reidel laughed. The laugh started in her mouth and ended in her mouth and involved no other organ or body part.

"With him? God no. We've got other fish to fry."

"I may be one of those fish," Remo said.

Wanda shrugged. "Can't make an omelet without a chicken somewhere being raped, love."

"I'm not worried about rape. I'm worried about being dead."

Wanda hmphhed. "You don't even know what dead is. Dead is when you have to wait for a seat in a restaurant. Dead is when they change their private numbers and you don't get them without asking. Dead is when suddenly everybody has a case of the outsies when you call. That's dead, honey. What do you know about dead? This town is all dead. There's just a few that stay alive and I'm going to be one of them. Gordons is going to help."

"You've got it wrong," Remo said. "Dead is when the flesh starts to turn black and becomes a banquet table for maggots. Dead is arms and legs ripped off and stuck in a wall. Dead is brains scooped out of skulls that look as if they were crushed by a steamshovel. Dead is blood and broken bones and organs that don't work. Dead is dead. And Gordons will help you do that, too."

"Are you threatening me, lover?" asked Wanda, looking into Remo's deep brown eyes that bordered on black and never imagining for an instant that Remo *would* kill her if he decided it would help stifle his next annoying yawn. He did not like this woman.

Remo smiled.

"No threats." He stood up and touched Wanda's bangled wrist with his right fingers. He pressed lightly. He smiled again and his eyes narrowed slightly and he moved his fingers again, and when he left the office a few minutes later, he had Wanda's assurance that she would notify him as soon as she heard from Mr. Gordons—and he had a date for Chiun to meet with Rad Rex. Wanda, still sitting behind her desk, for the first time that day did not feel like having anything to eat.

12

"I saw them," Chiun said.

"Yeah. Well, that's not important now. Mr. Gordons in in town. I've found it out for sure."

"Wait," said Chiun, raising a long bony finger for silence. "Just who is to say that this is not important? Do you alone decide what is important? Is that the way things are to be? After all the time and trouble I have gone to to teach you to be a human being? Now you say 'that is not important'?"

Remo sighed. "Who did you see?"

"I did not say I saw a who. I said I saw them."

"Right. Them. Who's them? Or what's them, if you prefer."

"I saw Doris Day's dogs."

"Gee. Wow. No fooling."

Pleased at Remo's display of interest, Chiun said,

"Yes, I saw them in the Beverly Hills. There were many of them. A woman was walking them."

"Was the woman Doris Day?"

"How would I know that? However, she was fair-haired and lissome, and it might have been she. It might have been. She moved like a dancer. It probably was Doris Day. Blonde. Lean. Yes, it was Doris Day. I saw Doris Day walking her dogs."

"I knew you'd see the stars if you took that bus ride."

"Yes, and I saw others. Many others."

Remo did not ask who, and Chiun did not volunteer any names.

"Are you all done now?" asked Remo.

"Yes. You may go on with your inconsequential report."

"Mr. Gordons is in town. We're his targets. And we've got a meeting with Rad Rex tomorrow. I figure that's when Gordons is coming after us."

"It is about time that you performed well some act of importance. When is it, this meeting?"

"At Global Studios. Five P.M."

"Five P.M.," said Chiun. "My bus ride for tomorrow is at four P.M. I will not be back in time."

"Then don't go."

"No. It is all right. I am accustomed to dealing with your ineptitude. I will take a different bus. It doesn't matter." He stopped in mid-sentence. Remo looked. Chiun was staring out the car window toward the sidewalk, where a group of pedestrians waited.

"Look, Remo. Isn't that . . . ?"

"No," said Remo. "It isn't."

145

13

"You understand? He will attempt to find you?"

"Here now," said Wanda Reidel. "Of course I understand. Who's the creative one here anyway?"

"Sadly, it is true," Mr. Gordons said. "I am not creative. You are. Forgive my presumptions."

"Of course."

"You must be sure that he does not find you. Then release the information on the computer sheets that I gave you. The way we discussed. He will look for you and that will separate him from the Oriental, with whom I will deal. Then I will destroy this Remo. And you will have the publicity that you think is helpful to your career."

"I understand all that," said Wanda impatiently. "This Oriental must be quite a man."

"He is," Mr. Gordons agreed. "Most unusual. He has no fear and no weakness that I have been able to discern. However, with the element of surprise, I will be able to destroy him. I will now make the telephone call."

Gordons dialed the phone next to the pool at Wanda's home in Benedict Canyon, one of the strips running from Hollywood to the sea, gouges in the earth, as if a giant had scratched his fingers through soft sand. As Gordons dialed, Wanda lay back on her beach chair, eating a bagel, rubbing Nubody cream over her skin.

"Is this the one called Smith? This is Mr. Gordons."

Gordons listened for a moment, then said: "It will do you no good to know where I am. I am calling to tell you that the computer report on the secret organization you command will be made available to the press of your nation."

Pause.

"That is correct. This will be done today at five P.M. by Ms. Wanda Reidel in her office. She will announce plans for a new motion picture about your secret government organization. It will star Rad Rex."

Pause.

"That is quite accurate, one called Smith. I am going to use all the confusion this creates to destroy the one called Remo and the old Oriental. It is a good plan, is it not? Creative?"

He listened for a moment, then yelled "nigger" and slammed the receiver back on its base.

Wanda Reidel stopped examining her naked pubis. "What's wrong? What did he say?"

"He said I had the creativity of a night crawler."

Wanda laughed, and Mr. Gordons glared at her.

"I would take that laughter to be mocking me if it were not for the fact that I require your services."

"Don't ever forget it, Gordons. Without me, you're nothing. I made you what you are today."

"Incorrect. The scientist at the space laboratories made me what I am today. You are trying to improve upon her work. That is all. I am leaving now, for there are things to do before I encounter the old one at five o'clock today."

And with a smooth gait, inhuman in its absolute uniformity, Gordons walked away, leaving Wanda at poolside. She was still there five minutes later when the telephone rang.

"Hello, love," she said.

"This is Remo. I thought you were going to tell me when you heard from Gordons. What's all this crap about a new movie?"

"It's true. All true."

"Why are you doing this?" said Remo.

"Because Gordons wants me to. And because I want to. It'll make me a household name. Everybody in this industry, television too, they'll be knocking down my door when this breaks. I'll be the . . ." She stopped and said, "Five o'clock today. At my office. And don't try to talk me out of it, because you can't. See you, love. Kiss, kiss."

She replaced the receiver with one outstretched finger. Remo hung up the phone at the Sportsmen's Lodge.

"Chiun, you're going to have to go see Rad Rex by yourself."

"I am old enough to travel alone."

"It's not the travel. There'll be a studio car. But I

won't be able to go. And Mr. Gordons has figured out a way to separate us."

"See," said Chiun. "It is as I have always said. Even bad machines sometimes do good deeds."

"Oh, go scratch. I hope he eats you. Turns you into engine oil."

"Not before I see Rad Rex. To think after all these years."

"The car'll come for you. I've got to go. To Wanda Reidel's. I'll catch up to you."

"Take your time," said Chiun. "I should have some moments of rest during the day."

Unless they were familiar ones, limousines meant absolutely nothing to Joe Gallagher, a day-shift guard at the front gate of Global Studios.

Nowadays anybody could rent a limousine, and some screwball groupies had been known to do just that. A half-dozen of them would pool their money, hide in the trunk, and then, when they got past an unsuspecting guard, park their rented rig someplace and go harass a star. That had happened just last month, and one of Hollywood's reigning cowboy heroes—one of those ten percent of stars whom Joe Gallagher did not also classify as a bastard—had been gang-raped by six young girls, and an inexperienced guard at the gate had been canned.

So Gallagher raised an imperious hand to halt the gray Silver Dawn Rolls Royce as it made the right-hand turn up the slight incline to the guard's booth. The uniformed driver lowered the window.

"A guest of Miss Wanda Reidel to see Rad Rex," the driver said. His voice sounded bored.

Gallagher peered in through the driver's window

and saw an old Chinaman sitting in the back seat, his hands folded calmly in his lap.

The old man smiled. "It is true," he said. "I am going to meet Rad Rex. It is true. Honest."

Gallagher turned away and rolled his eyes up into their sockets. Another nut.

He consulted a clipboard in his booth, then waved the driver past.

"Bungalow 221-B."

The driver nodded and started slowly inside the lot.

"A bungalow?" his passenger said. "For a big star like Rad Rex? Why a bungalow? Why not that big ugly building over there?" Chiun asked, pointing to a tall cube of a building, with black sunguard windows. "Who uses that building?"

"Nobodies use that building," said the driver. "Big shots use bungalows."

"This is very strange," Chiun said. "I thought in this country, the bigger and more important you are the bigger the building you have to have."

"Yeah, but this is California," said the driver as if that explained everything. And, indeed, it did.

Bungalow 221-B was in the back of the lot. Rad Rex was already there, wearing his doctor's smock, sitting at the makeup table in a large rear sitting-room/office and pouring out his tale of woe to the young man whom Wanda Reidel had sent over to be his escort around Hollywood.

"Is this silly or what?" asked Rad Rex. The younger man, a curly-haired brunet with cheeks so lively they seemed rouged, shrugged and raised his hands, palm-upwards, at his sides, a move which jangled his silver bracelets.

"I guess so, Mr. Rex."

"Call me Rad. It is. It is silly. I've come three thousand miles to meet a nobody who watches my stupid show. Have you ever seen my show?"

The young man hesitated a split second, unsure of what to answer. If he said no, he might offend this creep. If he said yes, and Rad Rex was serious in his disdain for people who watched his show, it might reduce him in Rad Rex's eyes.

The thought of the simple truth—that he watched Rad Rex's show only on infrequent occasions and then only to see if they were still hiring gays—never occurred to him.

"Afraid not," he said finally. "It's on when I'm working, you see."

"You haven't missed a thing. I play this doctor. Kind of a Marcus Welby with balls. Very big in the ratings."

"I know that. It's got to be very big for Ms. Reidel to handle you."

"Is Wanda your agent too?" said Rex.

The young man laughed self-deprecatingly. "No, no, but I wish she were. If she were, I bet I could get something better than walkons and clothes modeling."

Rex looked the dark-haired man up and down. "Yes, you look like a model. Your body's got the lines for it."

"Thank you, but I want to be an actor. A real actor, not just a star."

Rex turned back to the mirror and began putting a faint oil on his eyelashes with a Q-tip. The younger man realized he had offended him, that Rex probably had thought he was being insulted when

151

the youth talked about being an actor and not just a star, and the young man stepped forward and said, "Here, Rad, let me help you."

He took the Q-tip from Rad Rex, placed his left hand along the side of Rex's right cheek and began to stroke the oil gently on the actor's eyelashes to make them look longer and thicker.

Rex closed his eyes and leaned back in the chair.

"Maybe we could find a spot for you in my show. But you'd have to come to New York."

"I'd walk to New York for a spot in your show."

"I'll talk to Wanda about it."

"Thank you, Mr. Rex."

"Rad."

"Rad."

Knock, knock. The rapping reverberated through the room.

"That must be your guest."

"Isn't this terrible? Why me, Lord?" asked Rex.

"Because you're a star," the younger man cooed, patting Rex's cheek softly and then going to the front of the bungalow to open the door.

"Wait. Do I look all right?"

"You look lovely."

The dark-haired man opened the door and tried to contain his smile at the sight of the wizened old Oriental standing in front of him, wearing a black-and-red brocade kimono.

"Yes?" he said.

"You are not Rad Rex."

"No, I'm not. He's inside."

"I am to see him."

"Please come this way." The man led Chiun toward the back room, where Rex sat staring into the mirror, intently examining a nonexistent pimple over the left side of his mouth. He saw the Oriental in the mirror, and smoothing his medical coat over his hips, rose and turned with a slight smile.

"It is you, it is you," said Chiun.

"I am Rad Rex."

"You look just as you do on the picture box."

With a wink at the young man, Rad Rex said, "People are always saying that."

"I will never forget how you saved Meriweather Jessup from a life as a woman of the night."

"One of my better moments," said Rad Rex, still smiling.

"And the ease with which you cured the cocaine addiction of Rance McAdams was also most impressive."

As he spoke, Chiun rocked back and forth on his feet, like a young boy called into the principal's office for the first time in his school career.

"The difficult I do immediately. The impossible takes a little longer," conceded Rad Rex graciously.

"What do you think was your most famous case?" asked Chiun. "Was it your saving the unborn child of Mr. Randall McMasters? Or the emergency operation you performed on the husband of Jessica Winston, after she had fallen in love with you? Or the time when you found a leukemia cure for the lovely young daughter of Walker Wilkinson after she had gone into a depression over the death of her prize-winning colt?"

Rad Rex looked at Chiun with narrowed eyes. This was a setup. Maybe "Candid Camera." How did this old geezer know so much about a show whose

153

characters changed so fast the hardest thing an actor had to do was to keep the names straight? How did he remember names and incidents that Rad Rex had forgotten the moment after they had happened? It was a setup. Wanda Reidel had booked Rad Rex for "Candid Camera." Rex glanced at the dark-haired young man but saw nothing on his bland face. At least he wasn't in on it.

Rex decided if he was going to be on film, he'd better look good.

He ignored Chiun's questions. "I've told you my name, but you haven't told me yours."

"I am Chiun."

Rex waited for more, but nothing else was volunteered.

"Just Chiun?"

"It is enough of a name."

"Chiun? Chiun?" Rad Rex mused aloud, and then the name came back to him. "Chiun! Do you have an autographed picture of me?"

Chiun nodded in agreement, happy that Rad Rex had remembered.

Rex sat down cautiously. Maybe it wasn't "Candid Camera." Maybe this old guy was a front man for the Mafia, and they wanted to produce a picture. He had always thought you had to be Italian to be in the Mafia. Best to be cautious.

"Won't you please sit down and tell me something about yourself?" he asked.

"I think I'd better leave," the young dark-haired man said. "I'll see you later, Mr. Rex. Mr. Chiun."

Rex waved an impatient hand in dismissal. Chiun declined to acknowledge the young man's existence.

He sat in one smooth motion in a chair across from Rex's couch.

"I am Chiun. I am the Master of Sinanju. I am employed to make sure that the Consitution of the United Sates continues to fail to work in exactly the same way it has failed to work for two-hundred years. It is a most important job I have, and its only real reward is that it leaves my daytimes free to watch yours and other beautiful poems on the television."

"Very interesting," said Rad Rex. Who said you had to be sane to be in the Mafia? This ninny was probably the head of the Mafia's Far East office.

"What is your nationality?" Rad Rex asked shrewdly. Maybe the man had *some* Italian blood.

"I am Korean. There is an old story that when God first made man, he put the dough in the oven and..."

After Mr. Gordons had left her, Wanda Reidel snuggled down deeper into her leather-strapped beach chair and reached for more Nubody oil.

She poured a gob of it onto her right palm, replaced the bottle on the tile-topped table next to her, and began to rub the oil into her abdomen and down onto her thighs.

It was all right for Mr. Gordons to tell her to run away from Remo but that was because Mr. Gordons had not been in her office the day Remo showed up there. Mr. Gordons had not seen the look Remo had given her, had not felt his touch on her wrist. If Gordons had seen or felt that, he would have realized that this Remo posed no threat to anybody's plan. He was so hot for Wanda's body nothing else mattered to him.

She rubbed even bigger gobs of the cream into her elbows and knees and neck.

And why shouldn't Remo be? It was amazing the way most men fell all over themselves at the sight of a young, pretty woman and there was no shortage of that type in Hollywood. But that told you more about the man than about the woman. Those women were crap, just crap in Wanda's book, even though she had built a career on them. Crap. A real man wanted a real woman. How odd that someone like Remo, an outsider, could come to town and on first meeting recognize the real woman, the beauty that reposed beneath the mass of sinew, muscles, fat, suet, and lard that was Wanda Reidel.

And he had. She knew. She had seen that look.

So when Remo called soon after Mr. Gordons left, she did not bother to hide from him. Not really. And when Remo came, they would make wild magnificent love. She would allow him her body. And then the two of them would sit and they would make plans for the disposal of Mr. Gordons who had outlived—make that outlasted—his usefulness.

Wanda finished the oiling ritual and began to apply rouge to the mounds of her breasts and a slightly darker-than-natural skin makeup into the crevice between her breasts and around the bottom and sides of them.

She lifted each breast and examined it carefully as she worked, glad that no purplish veins were visible. She hated those young actresses with those breasts that stood up straight, pert and perky as their little bobbed noses.

Wanda's bosom could do the same thing if that was all she had to worry about during the day, just making sure her breasts were firm. But Wanda told herself that she was a working woman and didn't have time for such frills. Oh, for the day when she would be able to do nothing except exercise and keep her body lean and tan. And diet, too. Perhaps one of those all-protein diets. They seemed to work. She thought of cheese Danish and strawberry Danish and apple Danish and decided that when her great days of leisure came, protein diets were basically unhealthy. The body needed carbohydrate. Without carbohydrate, there was no blood sugar. Without blood sugar, resulting stupidity was followed immediately by death.

No. No fad diets for her. She would simply go onto a careful carlorie-counting regimen that she could be sure would be heathful and sound. There was no reason that a diet had to deprive you of all the things you liked. A diet was supposed to make you feel better, not miserable.

After her triumphant move into the New York television market, after that, she definitely would find time to diet.

And to exercise. But not tennis. She hated tennis. It was a mindless insipid game played by mindless insipid twits who just wanted to show off their young, lean, tanned bodies. Like an advertisement that they were all good in bed. As if the body alone had anything to do with that.

When Wanda had first come to Hollywood, she had been the part-time girlfriend of an assistant producer. Later, when she became well known on her own, he had said at a cocktail party that "screwing Wanda Reidel has all the excitement of a stroll through an unused railroad tunnel. All the excitement and half the friction."

The assistant producer was now working as the assistant manager of a restaurant in Sumter, South Carolina. Wanda had seen to that. But the remark had outlived his career. It was one of the crosses Wanda had had to bear. Often when making love to her, men—even men who wanted something from her—would stop in the middle and laugh and she knew what it was. That goddam railroad-tunnel crack. And it wasn't true. God, it wasn't true. She knew it wasn't true. She was warm and loving and tender and sensuous and worldly, and she would prove all that to Remo today when he arrived.

She continued oiling her body. She heard a throat cleared behind her.

Because of the silence of the approach, she knew it was Mr. Gordons returning.

"Don't get upset," she said without turning. "I was just getting ready to go, so cool it."

She hoped he would leave right away. She didn't want him there when Remo arrived. She didn't want Gordons in the way of the monumental orgy that she envisioned for Remo.

"Why don't you pick up and beat it, love?" she said, still without turning.

"Whatever you want, love."

The voice wasn't Mr. Gordons, but before Wanda could turn around in her chair the way she had planned, thinning out her middle by making it longer with a langorous stretch, before she could do that, she found herself being lifted, still in the

158

leather-strapped chair, and tossed into the deep end of the kidney-shaped purple-tiled pool.

She hit with a splat. The heavy-framed chair sunk away beneath her, and she floundered. Water got into her nose and eyes. She coughed. She could feel mucus running out of her nose, down her upper lip.

Through her teared vision, she saw Remo standing at poolside, looking down at her.

"You bastard," she sputtered as she moved toward the side of the pool. "For that, you'll never get into films."

"Ah well, another promising career shot to hell. Where are the papers?"

"Papers?" asked Wanda as she started to pull herself out of the pool. She stopped when Remo's leather-shoed foot pressed lightly on the top of her head.

"The computer papers. The secret organization you're going to make a movie of. Gordons gave them to you, remember?"

"Wouldn't you like to know, you wise bastard? They're going to be in the hands of the press in just an hour."

"Oh?" Remo pressed down with his foot. Wanda felt her hands slip from the smooth glazed tile and her head was again underwater. She opened her eyes. She saw black swirls drifting past her eyes like a ghostly vapor. That goddam eye makeup. It was running. It wasn't supposed to run. She'd do something about that.

The pressure lessened on her head, and she popped upward out of the water like a fishing bobber when the line below it has been snapped by a large fish.

"Where is it, dearest?" said Remo, leaning over poolside. "You may be getting a clue by now that I'm not fooling."

He smiled. It was the same smile he had smiled in her office, but this time she recognized it. It wasn't the smile of a lover; it was the smile of a killer. It was a professional smile. On a lover's face, it meant love because love was his job; on this man's face it meant death because death was his job.

"They're in my briefcase. Just inside the door," she gasped, frightened and hoping that Mr. Gordons would find a reason to come back.

Remo gave her a wait-there-awhile push under the water with his foot. She felt her toes hit bottom. She spluttered and splashed. By the time she had struggled back to the surface, Remo was trotting out of the house. He had a pile of papers in his arms and was looking through them.

"This is it. Where'd you have the copies made?"

"Mr. Gordons made them."

"How many?"

"I don't know. He gave me eight and the original."

Remo shuffled through the large stack of papers. "Seems right. Nine here. Any more? Stick one in the files at your office?"

"No."

"Press releases? About your new movie?"

Wanda shook her head. Her sparse hair, all the lacquer washed out of it, shook around her head like wet strands of rope.

"I always work verbally with the press. I'm going to do that today."

"Correction love. You *were* going to do that today."

As Remo walked by her again, he used his foot to press her head down under the surface of the water. He went to a large baker's oven in the rear of the patio, California's nouveau riche version of a barbecue, its only concession to American style being that the giant oven was set atop a mass of red bricks. He found an electric on-off switch, kicked it on, and opened the oven door. Inside gas jets flamed and began to bring a glow to ceramic imitation charcoal. He waited a few seconds until the fire was sizzling, then began to throw in the batches of computer paper, a few sheets at a time, watching them flare and burn orange in the bluish glow of the bottled gas.

When all the paper was in and burned, Remo took a poker, designed to look like a fencing sword, and shuffled up the ashes and incompletely burned clumps of blackened paper. They flashed into fire all over again. Remo stirred up the remainder, turned the oven onto high, and closed the door.

When he turned, Wanda Reidel was standing behind him. He laughed aloud.

Her skin was pasty and dry looking, because the unaccustomed dousing had washed off all the Nubody oil. Her breasts sagged, forming a perfect two-pointed tiara for her stomach which sagged too. Her hair hung in loose strands down around her face, a pasty mass of uncooked dough in which her eyes, shorn of makeup, looked like two unhealthy raisins. Her legs rubbed together from top of thigh to knee, even though her feet were apart.

She had a pistol in her hand.

"You bastard," she said.

Remo laughed again. "I saw this scene in a movie once," he said. "Your breasts are supposed to be straining against some kind of thin gauze, struggling to be free."

"Yeah?" she said. "I saw that movie. It was a doggo."

"Funny. I sort of liked it," Remo said.

"The ending didn't work. It needed a new ending. Like this one." Wanda raised the pistol in both hands up in front of her right eye, squinted down the barrel and took aim at Remo.

Remo watched her leg muscles, waiting for the tell-tale tensing that would announce she was ready to fire. The almost hidden muscles in her calves tightened.

Remo looked up.

"Die, you bastard," Wanda yelled.

Remo's right hand flashed forward. The sword-like poker moved out in front of him. Its point slammed into the barrel of the gun and Remo jammed it in, deep, just as Wanda pulled the trigger.

The hammer hit the shell casing, and the bullet, blocked by the poker from leaving the barrel, exploded, backwards, all over Wanda's face. She stumbled back, her face pulp. Her foot hit the wet edge of the pool and she stumbled back into the water, holding the pistol in a death grip, sword still protruding from the front. And then the gun and poker dropped away, under the water, and Wanda floated limply atop the pool like a dead fish, staring up toward Remo with eye sockets blown empty by the exploding gun.

"All's well that ends well," said Remo.

14

The conversation could have been dull, but it hadn't been, since the old man talked about the thing Rad Rex considered most important in the world. Rad Rex.

"But I must confess," Chiun said, "there is one aspect of your shows that I find distasteful."

"What's that?" asked Rex, truly interested.

"The excessive violence," said Chiun. "In shows of such rare beauty it is a terrible thing to let violence intrude."

Rex tried to think of what violence the old man might be talking about. He could remember no fights, no shootings. Dr. Witlow Wyatt ran the only absolutely bloodless operating room in the world, and the most violent thing he had ever done was tear up a prescription blank.

"What violence?" he finally asked.

"There was a show. A nurse struck you." He looked at Rad Rex carefully to see if the man would remember."

"Oh, that."

"Yes, precisely. That. It is a bad thing, this violence."

"But it was only a slap," said Rex, regretting almost instantly having said it. From the pained look on Chiun's face, he could understand how the old man might regard a slap as the equivalent of World War III.

"Ah yes. But a slap may lead to a punch. And a punch may lead to an effective blow. Before you know it, you will be dodging guns and bombs."

Rad Rex nodded. The old man was serious.

"Don't worry. If it ever happens again," he said, "I'll take care of her." The actor rose to his feet and assumed a karate stance, arms held high and away from his body. "One blow to the solar plexis and she will never strike a physician."

"That is the correct attitude," said Chiun. "Because you allowed her to deal you a bad blow. Badly done, badly aimed, badly stroked. It can only embolden her."

"When I get her, I'll fix her. Aaaah. Aaaah. Aaaah," shouted Rex, slashing imaginary targets with karate hand swords.

"I can break a board, you know," he said pridefully.

"That nurse did not look like a board," said Chiun. "She might strike back."

"She'll never have the chance," said Rad Rex. He wheeled on an imaginary opponent. Out darted his left hand, fingers pointed like a spear; over his head

165

came his right hand, crashing down as if it were an axe.

He saw a wooden pool cue in a rack in a far corner of the room and whirled toward it, yanking it from the rack. He brought it back and placed it between the end of the sofa and the dressing table, stared at it, took a deep breath, then slashed his hand down onto the cue, which obediently cracked and clattered to the floor in two pieces.

"Aaaah, aaaah, aaaah," he yelled, then smiled and looked at Chiun. "Pretty good, eh?"

"You are a very good actor," said Chiun. "Where I come from you would be honored for your skill as an artificer."

"Yeah, yeah. But how about my karate, huh?" Rad Rex went into another rapid series of hand slashes. "How about that?"

"Awe-inspiring," said Chiun.

The telephone rang before Rad Rex could show Chiun any more of his martial arts skill.

"Yes," said Rex.

The voice was a woman's but a strange woman's voice, ice-cold and iron-hard, with no regional inflection, with not even the touch of the old South that was popular in most parts of California among women who spent their worktime talking on the telephone.

"I am calling for Ms. Reidel. The set to which you are to take your visitor is ready now. You may take him there now. It is the set in back of the main building in the far corner of the lot. Do not tarry. Take him now."

Click. The caller hung up before Rad Rex could speak.

The actor grinned sheepishly at Chiun. "That's one of the things I hate about being in a new town. People herd you about like an animal."

"True," said Chiun. "Therefore one must never go to a new town. One must be at home everywhere."

"How to do that would be a secret worth knowing."

"It is simple," said Chiun. "It comes from inside. When one knows what he is inside, then everyplace he goes is his place and he belongs there. And thus no town is new because no town belongs to someone else. All towns belong to him. He is not controlled. He controls. It is the same with your little dance."

"Dance?" said Rad Rex.

"Yes. The karate hopping that so many of you people do."

"Greatest killing technique ever devised."

"From my son I could not stand such an incorrect statement," said Chiun. "But from you, because you are unskilled and know no better . . ." He shrugged.

"You saw what I did with that pool cue," Rex said.

Chiun nodded and rose slowly, his black-and-red robe seeming to rise with a will of its own.

"Yes. Karate is not all bad. It teaches you to focus your pressure on just one point, and that is good. Karate is a rifle shot instead of a shotgun. For that it is good."

"Then what's bad about it?"

"What is bad about it," said Chiun, "is that it does nothing but direct your strength. Nothing but focus your energy. So it is an exercise. An art is creative. An art creates energy where none existed before."

167

"And what is an art? Kung fu?"

Chiun laughed.

"Atemiwaza?"

Chiun laughed again. "How well you know the names," he said. "Game players always do. No, there is only one art. It is called Sinanju. All else is just a copy of a piece of a fragment of a thought. But the thought itself is Sinanju."

"I've never heard of Sinanju," said Rad Rex.

"Because you are a special man and you may need someday to defend yourself properly against the evil nurse, I will show it to you," said Chiun. "This is a gift not bestowed lightly. Most to whom Sinanju is shown never have a chance to remember it or to talk of it."

He lifted up the heavy end of the pool cue which Rex had cracked with the side of his hand. Chiun hefted it carefully before handing it to the actor, who held it out in front of him like a billy club.

"You remember how hard you swung your arm to crack the stick?" said Chiun. "That was the focus of your power. But the power did not come from karate. It came from you. You were as the sun and karate merely a lens that focused your power into a bright dot to shatter that stick. The art of Sinanju creates its own power."

"I'd like to see this Sinanju," said Rad Rex. It did not occur to him to doubt Chiun. Like most Westerners, he assumed anyone with slanted eyes was a martial arts expert, just as all Orientals assumed all Americans could build and fly rockets.

"You shall," said Chiun. He arranged the thick half of the pool cue in Rad Rex's hands. When he was done, the stick was vertical, its shattered end

168

pointed toward the floor, the rubber bumper on its fat end pointed toward the ceiling. It was held lightly by Rad Rex at about the middle of the shaft, between the fingertips of the left hand and right hand, like a young baby holding a training glass of milk.

"Remember how hard you swung to shatter the stick. That was karate. A dance," said Chiun. "And this is Sinanju."

Slowly he raised his right arm over his head. Even more slowly he brought his hand down. The side of his hand hit lightly into the rubber ring that cushioned the end of the cue stick.

And then, by God, the hand was through the rubber ring and moving downward and ... Jesus Christ ... the hand was moving slowly through the almost-petrified wood of the cue, cutting through almost like a rip saw, and Rad Rex felt the old man's hand pass between his fingertips holding the stick and there was a strange buzzing feeling, almost as if the actor were being electrically shocked. Then the buzz was gone, and the old man's hand continued moving slowly through the wood and then it was out, at the splintered bottom of the shaft.

Chiun looked up and smiled at Rad Rex, who looked down at his hands, then separated them, and each hand held half of the cue stick, sawed through along its length. Rad Rex looked at the stick, then gulped and looked at Chiun. His face was puzzled and fearful.

"That is Sinanju," said Chiun. "But having seen it, you must now forget that you have seen it."

"I'd like to learn it."

"Someday," Chiun smiled. "When you retire from

all else, perhaps. When you have years to spend, perhaps. But for now you do not have the time. Consider the demonstration a gift from me. In return for the gift you once gave me. The picture with your own name on it and an inscription to me."

Chiun had just reminded Rad Rex of something. He had wanted all day to ask the old man how he had gotten the Mafia to muscle Rad Rex into signing that photograph. He looked now at the bisected cue stuck in his hands and decided there was no point in asking.

He knew. He knew.

15

It was a sleepy frontier saloon. Several bottles of rotgut whiskey stood on the bar. Four round tables with chairs around them were poised, empty, as if awaiting the arrival of men after the spring round-up. Swinging doors led, not to the street, but to a large photograph of a street that was posted on a board outside the swinging door.

"Why am I here?" asked Chiun.

"I was told to bring you here," said Rad Rex.

"I do not even like Westerns," said Chiun.

"I don't know why you're here. I was told to bring you here."

"By whom?"

"By one of Wanda's assistants, one of those nameless, faceless zombies she's got working for her."

"Would you say mechanical?" asked Chiun.

"You bet," said Rad Rex and then was propelled toward the door of the empty set by Chiun.

"Quick," said Chiun, "you must go."

"But why? Why should . . ."

"Go," said Chiun. "It may not go well for you here and I would not deprive the world of the genius of 'As the Planet Revolves.' "

Rad Rex looked at Chiun again, then shrugged and walked out into the bright sunlight of the Global Studios lot. So the old man was a little nuts. Who wouldn't be from watching soap operas all day long?

Inside, on the set, Chiun pulled a chair away from a table and sat on it lightly.

"You may come out now, tin man," he called aloud. "You gain nothing by waiting."

There was silence, then the swinging doors at the entrance to the saloon opened wide and in walked Mr. Gordons. He wore a black cowboy outfit and a black hat. Silver-studded black boots adorned his feet, matched by the silver-studded black hat he wore. He had on two guns, white-handled revolvers slung low at his side.

"Here I am, gook," he said, looking at Chiun.

Chiun rose slowly to his feet. "You are going to shoot me?" he said.

"Reckon so," said Gordons. "Part of my new strategy. Separate you from the one called Remo and pick you off one at a time."

"You put such faith in your guns?"

"Fastest draw in the world," said Gordons.

"How like you?" said Chiun. "A being made of junk relying upon junk to do a man's work."

"Smile when you say that, pardner," said Gordons.

172

"Do you like my new way of speaking? It is very authentic."

"It could not help but be an improvement," said Chiun.

"Reach for your guns, mister," said Gordons.

"I have no guns," said Chiun.

"That's your tough luck, old timer," said Gordons, and with hands that moved in a blur, he flashed two guns from their holsters and fired at Chiun, who stood still across nine feet of floor, facing him.

The cab let Remo off in front of the driveway to Global Studios, and the first thing Remo saw was Guard Joe Gallagher in the watchbooth. The second thing he saw was a golf cart, used by messengers for deliveries on the lot, parked next to a car at the curb while a young messenger placed something into the trunk of the parked car.

Remo hopped aboard the golf cart, stepped on the gas, and it lurched forward past Gallagher's watch booth.

"Hi," Remo called, driving by.

"Hey, you, stop. Whatcha doing?" yelled Gallagher.

"You see my ball?" Remo called. "I'm playing a Titleist Four." And he was past Gallagher and onto the lot. But where was Chiun?

Up ahead Remo saw a familiar face and drove up to the man who was walking along, slowly shaking his head.

Remo pulled up in front of him and said, "Where's Chiun? The old Oriental?"

"Who wants to know?" said Rad Rex.

"Mister, you've got one more chance. Where's Chiun?"

Rad Rex rocked back on his heels and raised his hands in front of his chest. "Better not fool with me, buddy. I know Sinanju."

Remo took the front of the golf cart in both hands, twisted and ripped out a piece of the fiberglass the size of a dinner plate and tossed it to Rex.

"Is it anything like this?" he said.

Rex looked at the heavy slab of fiberglass, then pointed over his shoulder to the closed door of the sound set. "He's in there."

Remo drove off. Behind him Rad Rex followed him with his eyes. It looked like everybody knew Sinanju except Rad Rex. He did not think he liked being in a town of martial arts freaks. He was going back to New York, and if Wanda didn't like it, screw her. Hire somebody to screw her.

Inside the building, Remo heard shots. He jumped off the still-moving golf cart, opened the door and raced inside.

As he moved through the door, Mr. Gordons wheeled and fired at the movement.

"Duck, Remo," called Chiun, and Remo hit the floor, rolling, spinning toward a large crate on the floor. Two bullets hit the door behind him.

Remo heard Gordons' voice. "You will be next, Remo. After I have disposed of the old man."

"He's still kind of talky, isn't he, Chiun?" Remo called.

"Talky and inept," said Chiun.

Remo peered over the top of the wooden crate, just in time to see Gordons fire two more shots at

Chiun. The old man seemed to stand still, and Remo wanted to shout to Chiun to move, to duck, to dodge.

But the old man seemed only to twist his body slightly and Remo could see the sudden thuds of the fabric of his robe as the bullets hit it, and Chiun called: "How many bullets, Remo, have those guns?"

"Six each," Remo yelled back.

"Let's see," said Chiun. "He has fired nine shots at me and two at you. That is eleven and leaves him one more."

"He fired three at me," Remo said. "He's out of ammunition."

"Eleven," Chiun called.

"Twelve," yelled Remo. He stood up and again Gordons wheeled and squeezed the trigger at Remo.

Bang! The gun fired but Remo moved on the flash of light, before the sound, and the bullet hit the wooden box, gouging out a large slash from it.

"That's twelve now," said Remo.

"Then I will destroy you with my hands," Gordon said. He dropped both guns on the floor and advanced slowly toward Chiun, who backed off and began circling, away from Gordons and away from Remo, opening Gordons' back for Remo.

Remo moved forward, between the box and the wall, toward the old Western saloon set.

His hand brushed something as he moved, and he looked down and saw a fire extinguisher on the floor. He grabbed it up in his right hand, and came forward.

Chiun had continued circling and now was almost over Gordons' guns. In one smooth movement, he scooped up both revolvers.

"They are expended, gook," Gordons said. He circled, keeping his eyes on Chiun, and Remo moved up behind him until he was only five feet away.

"No weapon is useless to the master of Sinanju," said Chiun. He twirled both guns in the air above his hand, seemed ready to unloose the gun from his left hand, then let fly the gun from his right hand.

It buried itself deep in Gordon's stomach, but there was no sparking, even though the force of the projectile had penetrated the hard wall of the abdominal cavity.

"His circuit controls are somewhere else, Chiun," said Remo.

"Thank you for telling me what I have just learned," said Chiun.

"It will do you no good," said Gordons. He moved a step closer to Chiun. "This is your end, old man. You will not evade me as you evade my bullets."

"And you can't evade me," said Remo. He turned the fire extinguisher upside down. There was a faint chemical hiss. Gordons spun toward Remo, just as Remo squeezed the handle and a heavy white foam spritzed out of the extinguisher and swallowed up Gordon's face. As he turned, Chiun unleashed the second gun, firing it, like a deadly frisbee, end-over-end into the heel of Gordons' right foot.

There was an immediate sparking. Gordons' hands reached up to claw the foam from his eyes, even as Remo fired more at him.

And as he watched, Gordons' hand movements grew slower and slower and his heel continued to spark against the revolver imbedded deep in it and then Gordons said:

"You can not escape me," but each word came out

slower than the word before it until "me" sounded like "mmmeeeeeeeee," and the android dropped onto the floor at Remo's feet.

"Bingo," said Remo. He continued spraying Gordons until the whole body was covered in a mound of thick white chemical foam, then he tossed the empty fire extinguisher into the corner behind him.

Chiun stepped forward and touched Gordons' prone body with a toe. There was no reflex movement.

"How'd you know the circuits were in his heel?" asked Remo.

Chiun shrugged. "The head was too obvious. Last time it was the stomach. This time, I decided, the foot. Particularly since I had seen him limp at the hospital."

"This time, we get rid of him," said Remo who looked around until he found a fire axe on the wall and began chopping into the mound of foam, sending splatters ceilingward, feeling like an axe murderer and he dissected Mr. Gordons into a dozen pieces.

"Hold," said Chiun. "It is enough."

"I want to make sure it's dead," said Remo.

"It is dead," said Chiun. "Even machines die."

"Speaking of machines," said Remo. "We've got to get Smith loose."

"It will be nothing," said Chiun.

16

Chiun freed Smith by long-distance telephone from the Sportsmen's Lodge.

On the way back to the lodge, he had Remo stop in a drugstore and buy a simple bathroom scale.

In their room, he directed Remo to call Smith.

"Tell the emperor to have a scale brought into his room," Chiun directed. He waited while Remo transmitted the message and then waited some more while Smith got on a scale.

"Now tell him to find his weight," said Chiun.

"One hundred forty-seven pounds," Remo said to Chiun.

"Now tell him to put ten pounds of weight into each pocket of his kimono and to walk from the room," said Chiun.

Remo passed along the message.

"Are you sure this will work?" asked Smith.

"Of course it will work," said Remo. "Chiun hasn't lost an emperor yet."

"I'll call you back if it works," said Smith and hung up.

Remo waited by the phone as seconds turned to minutes.

"Why doesn't he call?" he asked.

"Do something productive," said Chiun. "Weigh yourself."

"Why? Is this room mined too?"

"Put your feet upon the scale," ordered Chiun. Remo weighed one hundred fifty-five.

The needle had barely stopped jiggling when the telephone rang.

"Yeah," said Remo.

"It worked," said Smith. "I'm out. But now what? We can't leave the room mined."

"Chiun, he wants to know now what," said Remo.

Chiun looked out the window at the small trout stream.

"Have him prepare weights of one hundred forty-seven pounds for him, one hundred fifty-five pounds for you, and ninety-nine pounds for me," said Chiun. "He should put these weights on rollers, roll them all into the room, and stand back from the force of the boom boom."

"He'll do it after he gets bomb experts there," Remo told Chiun after passing along the message.

"How he does it is of no concern to me," said Chiun. "I do not bother myself with details."

The next morning, Smith called to announce that the plan had worked. The room had exploded, but that section of the hospital had been evacuated and with heavy explosion-resistant mesh and padding,

Smith's experts had been able to contain the blast with little damage and no injuries.

"Thank Chiun for me," said Smith.

Remo looked at the back of Chiun, who was watching his daytime soap operas. "As soon as I get a chance," he said.

Later that day, he told Chiun of Smith's success.

"Of course," said Chiun.

"How did you know it was mined to explode by our weights?" asked Remo.

"I asked myself how you would set such a boom boom. I answered myself, Remo would do it with weights. What other way, then, would another uncreative creature do it?"

"That's your final word on the subject?" asked Remo.

"That word is sufficient," said Chiun.

"Go scratch," said Remo.

When they left Hollywood the next day, Remo managed to drive his car into a long line of limousines cruising slowly along with their headlights turned on in broad daylight.

He pulled out of the line, up alongside a car, and called to the driver: "What's going on?"

"Wanda Reidel's funeral," the man called back.

Remo nodded. In the rearview mirror, he saw the limousines stretched out behind him for almost a mile.

"Big crowd," he called to the driver.

"Sure is," the driver called back.

"Just proves what they always say," said Remo.

"What's that?"

"Give the people something they want to see and they'll come."